I hadn't looked for Quinn.

Not really.

I may have typed his name into a google search a couple of times. I might even have looked for people named Quinn on Facebook.

But Quinn and business had yielded nothing but pages and pages of strangers. I didn't even know where he was from.

Besides, what would I do if I did happen across him? It would have only hurt me to see that he'd moved on with his life. As he should have.

I was the one who had insisted that we not disclose our last names.

I kept thinking that I couldn't do that to him.

He would have wanted to stay together and I was entering a way of life that I couldn't in all fairness subject him to.

Any future we would have had wouldn't have been fair to him.

Quinn had been one of the top business students in the country at the same time I was.

My gaze flicked down to our hands. To his left hand.

There was no ring on his left hand.

That didn't mean anything.

I tried to steady my heart rate. I felt like I was coming out of an aileron roll.

"How are you here?" I asked.

A slow grin spread across his face.

"I think that's the question I should be asking you," he said. "You're a pilot?"

I nodded.

"How is that possible?" he asked.

I shrugged. "Air Force."

He looked at me sideways.

"Wait a minute," he said, pulling me with him to sit across from him in the chair I'd just vacated.

He sat forward, not letting go of my hands, searching my eyes.

It was as though if he let go of me I would disappear.

"Before," he said. "Ten years ago. Were you Air Force?"

"I was ROTC," I said. "so yes."

"Then... why?"

I knew what he was asking.

He wanted to know why I wouldn't tell him who I was. How to stay in touch with me.

"Because," I said, looking toward the window. Toward the Houston skyline and the majestic full moon behind it.

He'd been here in Houston all along.

SECOND CHANCE DESTINY

ALSO BY KATHRYN KALEIGH

Contemporary Romance

The Worthington Family

The Heart of Christmas

The Magic of Christmas

Second Chance Kisses

Second Chance Secrets

First Time Charm

Three Broken Rules

Second Chance Destiny

Unexpected Vows

Billionaire's Unexpected Landing

Billionaire's Accidental Girlfriend

Billionaire Fallen Angel

Begin Again

Love Again

Falling Again

Just Stay

Just Chance

Just Believe

Just Us

Just Once

Just Happened

Just Maybe

Just Pretend

Just Because

SECOND CHANCE DESTINY

THE WORTHINGTONS

KATHRYN KALEIGH

SECOND CHANCE DESTINY

PREVIEW: UNEXPECTED VOWS

Written by Kathryn Kaleigh

Published by KST Publishing, Inc., 2022

Cover by Skyhouse24Media

www.kathrynkaleigh.com

To learn more about Kathryn Kaleigh, visit

www.kathrynkaleigh.com

Kathryn Kaleigh

1

NOELLE WINSTON

"Prepare for landing."

The pilot's abrupt command was followed by the flight attendants making one last run through the aisle before taking their seats near the cockpit and buckling in.

Houston's George Bush Intercontinental Airport. Both my mother and father still called it Houston Intercontinental Airport. Though the airport was renamed when I was a child, I had no memory of it being called anything other than George Bush Intercontinental Airport.

The plane's speed slowed to stabilize the approach and the airplane continued its three-degree angle as it approached the runway. The flaps extended and the spoilers were activated to increase drag.

Ten years.

Ten years since I had been home.

In some ways, I hardly even felt like the same person.

In other ways, it felt like I'd only left yesterday and everything I'd done and experienced in between faded away into a distant memory. Nothing more than a dream.

The pitch of the plane's motor increased as the pilot made

adjustments. Either it was windy or the pilot was inexperienced.

It was a cool, crisp October day. Friday afternoon.

We made the final descent, gliding over clusters of homes in subdivisions. We were flying low enough to see the outline of swimming pools in the backyards.

As we flew over the interstate, I leaned back against the seat and checked my seatbelt. It seemed worthless compared to the five-point harness I was used to.

I pulled out my air pods and slipped them into my ears.

I didn't listen to music. I liked it quiet.

Besides, I had to prepare myself for my interview with Skye Travels.

Skye Travels was an up and coming private airline. I didn't remember it from when I lived in Houston ten years ago, but I hadn't been focused on the world of aviation at the time. In addition to my course work, my activities in the ROTC Silver Wings program had kept every minute of my days more than occupied.

Until I'd taken those two weeks off at the end of my last semester and before I reported to duty.

According to my quick dive on the Internet, Skye Travels had cornered the market on private airlines in Houston.

They also had planes scattered all across the country. Dallas. Mackinac Island. Denver. From what I'd read, Noah Worthington even started the company in Dallas. I was curious about the history of the company, but that would probably require asking someone who worked there. Maybe even Noah Worthington himself.

The wheels touched down in a remarkably smooth landing as the pilot switched to reverse thrust.

The cabin shook and people silently braced themselves.

I sat quietly, mentally going through the motions involved in bringing a plane to the ground, then taxing along the tarmac.

For most passengers, the flight was over. But I knew how much work the pilots still had to do before the doors opened.

I had no reason to be nervous. I was a seasoned air force pilot who'd logged an enormous number of flight hours.

But not in the civilian world.

There was a chance that Noah wouldn't hire me for that reason. It took a different skill set to fly passengers from point A to point B while catering to their whims than it did to fly a fighter jet.

I was the daughter of a full bird colonel—retired, so I hadn't grown up anywhere in particular. But I'd spent five college years in Houston… the longest I'd lived anywhere. So that made me think of Houston as home.

I didn't know anyone here. I wasn't the kind of girl who had girlfriends. I had work friends, but they changed regularly along with my location.

If I didn't get this job with Skye Travels, I would have to pick somewhere else to apply. It probably hadn't been smart to put all my eggs in one basket, especially since I didn't have a backup plan. No clue where else I would want to live other than Houston.

It wasn't like I needed a job—not for money. I was getting full Air Force retirement. But the thought of having endless days with no purpose gave me hives.

I needed to work and since flying was my life, it made sense that I would apply to work as a pilot. I didn't have the certifications to apply for commercial jobs. That was okay. I honestly didn't think a commercial job would keep me busy enough.

The plane came to a stop and ninety percent of the passengers jumped out of their seats. It wasn't like they could anywhere until it was time.

I sat calmly in my seat and waited. The flight wasn't over until the doors opened and it was my turn to exit the plane.

All those people standing impatiently did nothing to speed things along.

I pulled out my phone and switched it from airplane mode.

With retirement, even at thirty-four, my phone had gone noticeably quiet. Not having any responsibilities meant not having any messages or calls. I had no friends to speak of and other than my parents, I had no family. My parents stayed in Germany after my father retired. We'd never been close, and now, with them living halfway across the world, we had even less need to stay in touch with each other.

I had nothing against them. They did their thing and I did my thing. With both my father and me being military, our schedules rarely allowed for family time.

That might change now that we were both retired.

Retired. Such an odd word for me to be using to describe myself.

If I had anything to do with it, my so-called retirement was going to last about half a minute.

All I had to do was to convince Noah Worthington to hire me to fly for him.

Then I could settle into a job that would keep my sufficiently busy in the city that held my fondest memories.

It wasn't too much to ask. A meaningful job. A place to call home.

2

QUINN WORTHINGTON

Buried beneath paperwork again.

Soothing classic music spilled out of the phone sitting on my desk and beneath the music was another layer—the heavy sound of jets coming and going.

I gave my eyes a rest and picked up my cup of coffee, almost too cold to drink.

As the youngest of five children to airline mogul Noah Worthington, I'd found my way to the position of Vice-President of Skye Travels.

My father, Noah Worthington, was of course, president and would be until the moment he died. I was content to be vice-president, but I wanted more out of the position than merely being a paper-pusher. I was making progress in adding PR to my position.

At thirty-five, I already had more responsibility than most people my age. Despite what people liked to assume—since I was the owner's son—I'd worked my way up from the bottom.

As far as I was concerned, it was a good use of my business degree.

Anytime I thought it might not be challenging enough, all I

had to was to wait a minute for Noah to give me some new and challenging task.

Unfortunately, most those tasks involved paper in some way or another.

Despite cutting my teeth in the air, I'd never had a desire to be a pilot. Learning about engines and aerodynamics and everything aviation had never captured my passion.

I liked business. So no matter my complaints, I loved my job.

I pushed back in my chair and looked out over the tarmac. The only person who had a better view was my father. But I could see everything I needed to see.

The tarmac was just fine. And on days like today I knew I had at least a little bit of my father in me.

It was Friday afternoon on a crisp October day. I watched in wonder as one of the big commercial jets lifted itself off the ground. I didn't need to know the hows and whys to find it fascinating.

Skye Travels had their own area at a corner of the airport. We shared it with other private planes, but for all intents and purposes, we claimed it.

Noah was interviewing a pilot today. I didn't know who. It didn't matter to me until he signed them up. Then I went to work. It was my job to teach them how to use the computer program where everything happened from flights to paydays. If they didn't learn to use the system, they didn't get paid.

For some reason, pilots found it challenging. For me, it was simple.

My father strode out the back door toward the Cessna Citation sitting outside the hangar. The bright red Skye Travels logo was splashed across the tail.

My father was an eccentric man. He could afford to be. He'd taken an idea and nurtured it into a thriving business. A man to be envied to be sure.

His eccentricity manifested itself primarily in his relationships with his pilots.

He'd been known to open satellite services in states in order to keep pilots with the company. He had two pilots based out of Mackinac Island right now.

Every time Father did these things, he just added another layer of wealth to his empire. And another layer of paperwork to my job.

Father also had interesting ways of interviewing pilots. A way that made the businessman in me cringe. As his son, I just shrugged it off. It seemed to work. Noah only hired the best.

Sometimes he just met with them and had a friendly conversation about nothing in particular in his office.

Sometimes he had them fly for him.

Either way, I was pretty sure he knew who he was going to hire before he ever laid eyes on them.

Father reached the airplane and opened the door. It looked like today was going to be one of those times when the interviewee got to pilot a plane for him.

Interesting. Sometimes I'd like to be inside my father's head to see just how he made his business decisions.

After hiring pilots, Father often brought them to our weekly family dinners, often with interesting ramifications. Two of my four sisters had married pilots Father had introduced them to.

We'd had a couple of female pilots working for us over the years. Father never brought them home. It made me wonder if he didn't introduce my sisters to certain pilots on purpose.

I wouldn't put it past him.

At any rate, the fact that he never brought the female pilots around led me to believe that he respected my wishes.

I didn't date and I'd made that clear to my family.

It wasn't that I didn't like women.

On the contrary.

It was just that there was one particular girl who had stolen my heart.

It had been a ridiculously long time ago… ten years, but I had not changed my mind.

Her name was Noelle and she was the girl I was going to marry.

All I had to do was to find her again.

3

NOELLE

Stepping off the elevator into the third-floor office space of Skye Travels, I was greeted by their logo splashed across the wall in front of me.

The lobby area to the left was large and spacious. Comfortable air chairs and a couple of sofas that were nicer than most people had in their homes.

Wearing high heels that I was most definitely not used to, I walked toward the receptionist, dragging my one suitcase behind me. I was accustomed to the whole flight suit attire including boots—flat boots.

In fact, this interview had sent me shopping for the kind of clothes I'd had no need for… well… since ever. I'd gone from being a college student to being in uniform.

"Hi." The receptionist smiled when I approached her desk.

Her name tag identified her an Jan.

"I'm here for an interview," I said. "with Noah Worthington."

"He's expecting you," she said.

I certainly hoped so, but the relief was involuntary. I waited for her to instruct me on where I should wait.

"He asked that you meet him on the tarmac," she said, glancing down at my suitcase. "You can leave that here."

Then she answered the phone and turned her attention to her computer.

"Okay," I said, but Jan had already dismissed me.

When I didn't move, she glanced at me and pointed in the general direction of the tarmac.

I went to the window and looked down.

A little Cessna Citation sat there with the door open.

Seemed a little backwards to me, but I was certain he had a reason for showing me one of his planes before the interview. Maybe the plane was about leave.

Either way, it was interesting. I could fly that little Cessna in my sleep.

Not one to question authority, I left my suitcase behind Jan and went back down the elevator. Apparently I was on my own in finding my way out to the tarmac. Very unusual. I hadn't been in the private sector since college.

Maybe things had changed.

Or maybe it was just Noah Worthington. One of the things, besides being based in Houston, that had attracted me to Skye Travels was Noah himself. When I'd mentioned his name to some of the guys who kept up with the private sector of aviation, they'd all said the same thing.

Noah only hired the best and he took a personal interest in his people.

No one had said anything to prepare me for the way this particular interview was going.

Stepping off the elevator and heading toward what looked like a back door, I squared my shoulders.

I could be flexible. Being in the military hadn't taken all the flexibility out of me.

I pushed open the door to the familiar scent of jet fuel coming in on the autumn breeze.

One thing hadn't changed. I loved Autumn.

Autumn held a special place in my heart.

Since the airplane had the Skye Travels logo splashed across the tail, I had to assume that I was supposed to meet Noah there.

The man who came to the door of the plane as I walked up matched the pictures I'd seen.

But something about his sideways grin looked familiar.

I quickly dismissed it. This wasn't the time or place for thinking about such memories. Using the strong mental will power I'd developed in the military, I set the memories aside.

"Thought we'd take this plane up for a spin," Noah said. "You wanna drive?"

4

QUINN

After going to the break room to get a fresh cup of coffee, I came back to stand at the window in my office.

Looks like today's interviewee was one of the lucky ones who got to fly as part of the interview. Lucky being relative.

As far as I knew that wasn't standard in the industry, but it didn't matter. As the owner of a private company, Noah could do whatever he wanted to do.

If he wanted to have them do loops in the air, he could do it.

The hot coffee burned my tongue as I watched the girl walking across the tarmac.

She was dressed to the nines. Tight pencil skirt. High heels.

The girl obviously had no idea that she was going to be flying today.

I could only see her from the back, but it was enough to tell me that she had a sexy figure and had long brown hair that fell in loose curls down her back.

She most definitely hadn't planned on flying.

My father was a wily one.

I sipped my coffee, more carefully this time, and rested my right forearm against the side of the window.

As Noah and the girl talked, he swept a hand in my direction.

The girl turned and looked at me.

Busted. Owning it, I raised a hand.

The girl raised a hand back to me. I couldn't see her face behind the reflective sunshades, but she was obviously attractive.

I sighed and turned away. There had been a few times like this over the years. A few times when I questioned my resolve.

And truth be known, my sanity.

What kind of sane man made a promise to a girl he'd only known for two weeks?

A promise that he would wait for her.

I will find you.

But how did a man find a girl whose last name he didn't know?

Tell me your last name.

She'd looked into my eyes and smiled a sad little smile.

It wouldn't be fair to you. Don't wait for me.

I'd busted the Internet upside down and back to find a girl named Noelle.

My Noelle.

I'd spent hours scouring social media. I'd even tried going through the university to find her. I'd shown up at what would have been her graduation, but apparently, the University of Houston was not her university. There was no Noelle on the program.

But either she didn't use social media or her accounts were well hidden.

I sighed and sat down at my desk.

How could a girl like her just disappear off the face of the earth?

There was a possibility that Noelle wasn't her real name.
If that was the case, I would never find her.
But that would be admitting defeat.
And I wasn't ready for that.

5

NOELLE

"Where are we going?" I asked as I went through the preflight checklist.

"Mackinac Island," Noah said. "I have to make a pick up."

I nodded. I'd quickly slipped off my heels and changed into a pair of flats I kept in my handbag. It was one of the practical habits I'd formed while in the service.

Noah sat next to me in the cockpit, no doubt watching everything I did.

Since this was a nontraditional interview, he no doubt had cues he watched for that would tell him whether or not I was right for the job.

Like a passion for flying.

A pilot would never turn down the opportunity to fly. They invented reasons all the time. Sometimes just to hop in a plane and fly somewhere for lunch.

So flying up to Mackinac Island to pick someone up was as good an excuse as any to be flying.

And it was a good excuse to see me in action.

He'd already filed the flight plan, so I checked the information in the plane's computer.

Everything looked good to go.

"Have you ever been?" he asked. "To Mackinac Island?"

"Unfortunately, no," I said. "But Somewhere in Time is one of my favorite movies."

Out of the corner of my eye, I saw the smile that crossed Noah's features.

Good. We'd made a connection there.

We needed three points of connection. One down. Two to go.

We had plenty of time. Between two and three hours just to get there.

Personally, I would have scheduled a shorter flight with an interviewee.

It was possible, of course, that he'd gotten in a bind with his scheduling.

"This is one of the best times to visit," he said. "The leaves will be changing."

"That sounds nice," I said. "I have a special affinity for Fall anyway."

"It's my favorite, too," he said.

Point two, maybe. But the weather and seasons didn't usually count. Not deep enough.

I started the taxi toward the runway and abiding by the Sterile Cockpit Rule, focused completely on getting the plane in the air.

Checked with flight control.

Did everything by the book.

Noah seemed pleasant enough.

Professional definitely.

He had quite the reputation to live up to.

His business was on one those lists the magazines put out. *Best entrepreneur. The one to watch.* And a host of others I couldn't remember right off.

There were a lot of reasons a pilot would want to work for

Skye Travels and it wasn't just because it was based in Houston.

My takeoff was smooth. No problems.

We leveled off at altitude and Noah settled back, looking relaxed. I would follow his lead on making conversation.

If he wanted to take a quiet ride up to Mackinac Island, it suited me just fine.

I'd just gotten to Houston and I was headed somewhere else.

It seemed to be the story of my life.

From childhood on, it seemed like I was always going somewhere. Moving somewhere new.

I just wanted to settle into one place.

I hoped it could be Houston.

But if not Houston, I would find someplace else.

The country was a big place and the world was even bigger.

6

NOELLE — BEFORE

The hotel conference room was oversized. The hotel itself was oversized.

To get to this particular conference room, from my hotel room, I'd taken an elevator and two escalators.

I was the first one to arrive, but that didn't last long.

It was early, so there was coffee and orange juice on tables against the back wall along with fruit cups and muffins. Something for those who wanted to eat healthy and something for those who didn't.

I'd already eaten.

I'd had room service sent up an hour ago. I'd ordered a breakfast of eggs, bacon, and hashbrowns. Toast and jelly included.

I'd stopped for a latte on the way here—this cavernous hotel had everything—so I had my own coffee.

I was nervous. My name tag had my first name only. Noelle. That was it. No other identifying information. And according to the rules and regulations of the program, that was all we were allowed to go by.

Only one hundred people from around the country were

chosen to participate in this selectively elite program for top scoring business students.

Completion of the program guaranteed participants a job just about anywhere.

But not only was it difficult to get accepted, it was hard to stay in.

The program had a ninety percent attrition rate. So out of the one hundred people chosen for the program, only ten would complete it.

It was only open to graduating senior at colleges around the states.

Applications had gone in over two years ago.

I'd sent it and forgotten about it.

Since that time I'd gotten super involved in ROTC and all I knew about my future was that I was going into the Air Force as a Lieutenant.

But when I got the letter to attend what they were calling a business internship program, I saw no choice but to accept.

I was far too competitive and ambitious not to.

Even if it didn't pay off immediately, I would have it on my resume.

It was one of the achievements that stayed with a person for a lifetime.

All I had to do was to keep from being one of the ninety people who were kicked out.

I wasn't afraid. Just nervous.

If I got kicked out, so what? It didn't change where I was headed.

Other students filed in and took their seats. Every day there would be fewer and fewer seats in the room.

From what I could find out, ten people would find letters inside their hotel rooms at the end of the day excusing them from the program.

By the end of the ten days, there would be ten people left.

That was just about all I knew about the two-week program.

I planned to get through it one way or another.

A guy sat down right next to me.

There were plenty of places to sit. I didn't know why he sat so close.

"Hi," he said. "I'm Quinn."

"Hi Quinn," I said, with a glance over in his direction.

He was what I called a preppy guy. Designer clothes. Classic. Understated. Short haircut. Good teeth.

This program was supposed to put us all on equal footing. We were to leave our background behind.

Hence, no last names were allowed. In fact, disclosing one's last name was automatic dismissal from the program.

"This should be interesting," he said, taking a sip of his coffee.

"I don't think we're supposed to talk to each other," I said.

"Probably not," he said. "but without some interaction, it's going to be a really long two weeks."

"It'll be even shorter if you get kicked out," I said.

He crossed one leg over the other in a casual, nonchalant move.

Quinn looked like any other college senior. Average height. Lean. Normally I would have just blown him off, but there was something about his eyes. They had a happiness to them that most guys... most people didn't have.

It was hard to ignore.

"We still get out of class for two weeks, though, right?"

He was grinning at me now.

So he was one of those. One who didn't take this whole program seriously.

That told me that this program wouldn't affect his future one way or another.

It probably wouldn't affect mine, either, but failing wasn't optional—at least not through overt negligence on my part.

"I don't know," I said. "probably. Does that mean you don't care one way or the other?"

"Oh no," he said. "I have my reasons for wanting to make it through."

"Well," I said, looking over at his name tag. I don't know why I thought it would tell me something he hadn't already told me. "Quinn. Here's hoping we both make it through to the end."

"We will," he said.

I didn't disagree. But I wanted inside his head.

"What makes you so sure?" I asked.

"Call it a hunch," he said.

The folder on the table in front of me blurred.

I had a hunch, all right. I had a hunch Quinn was going to turn my life upside down.

If I let him.

It was a good thing I had a solid wall of fortitude.

7

NOELLE

The island below was ablaze in oranges, yellows, and reds. A pop of color in the middle of a lake that looked more like an ocean.

Noah had been right. Fall on Mackinac Island was a sight to behold.

"That's the Grand Hotel," Noah said. "Longest porch in the world."

I recognized the setting for Somewhere in Time immediately.

So far the flight had been uneventful.

I'd decided that Noah was testing my ability to pivot.

It was an important quality in a good employee, especially a pilot.

And Noah only hired the best.

I was good at that. I could be up and ready to go anywhere at a moment's notice.

Mackinac had no flight control tower on site. I was getting information from the control tower in Cheboygan.

According to my instruments, there were crosswinds that the fellow in Cheboygan wasn't aware of.

I adjusted for a steeper approach. Engaged full flaps.

Noah wasn't saying anything. Just watching the instruments and my adjustments.

With a plane this light, most pilots would choose to divert to another airport. Cut their losses.

But I'd made enough crosswind landings that I was confident that I could get us safely to the ground.

After some mental calculations, I made the split-second decision to slightly angle the aircraft across the runway.

I was taking this plane down for a landing. Noah's presence faded into the background as I made the necessary adjustments.

The wheels touched the ground in a smooth landing—as smooth as any. If we'd had passengers, they wouldn't have a clue that this had been anything other than a regular landing.

I taxied over to the little airport building, my adrenalin coming down to earth along with the airplane.

As the airplane came to a stop, I looked over at Noah.

"Nice landing," he said.

I was pretty sure that was an understatement. It was some of my better work and I'd done it while under the pressure of a job interview.

If I hadn't known just how impossible that was, I would have thought that Noah had set this up on purpose.

The weather, of course, couldn't be manipulated. Not even for a man as powerful as Noah Worthington.

"Stand up for a minute if you like," he said. "I'll be right back."

Noah unbuckled, slipped out of the plane, and headed toward the terminal.

I took my time disembarking.

The breeze coming off the lake—the same breeze that had caused me trouble with my landing—was soft and cool.

Unlike the balmy southern air I'd just left, the air here

was dry.

I walked toward the edge of the runway to the stand beneath a row of red maple trees. A red so bright they looked like they were on fire.

I mentally added Mackinac Island to my list of places I wanted to spend a week.

Flying in and out of a place was like dropping in on a snapshot. The leaves moved and the wind brushed my skin. I could even hear the sound of a ferry horn wailing in the distance.

But some places, like this one, begged for more time.

I wanted to do more than drop in on a snapshot. I wanted to spend at least some time there—getting to know the culture... the history... taste the food.

Live for a moment in their shoes. What must it be like to live here on this island where winters were so bad they went weeks without leaving?

Where the lake froze over enough that cars could drive from the island to the mainland.

Although I wasn't from anyplace in particular, I'd grown up mostly in the south.

We'd spent only one year in Montana at the Malmstrom Air Force Base in Great Falls, Montana. Now that had been an interesting winter. I'd learned to snow board and make snow angels.

I'd had my first kiss on a freezing cold Friday night after a football game.

That was when my fondness for fall really started.

They could do away with all the other seasons and I would be just fine with it.

A few minutes later Noah came walking out with a tall surly looking teenage girl wearing a hoodie, the hood over her head, carrying a backpack.

We weren't picking up a what, but a who.

8

QUINN

I stayed late. Waiting for Father and his applicant to return from Mackinac Island.

Out of curiosity I'd made the effort to look up their flight plan. I just glanced at it see where they were headed and what time they were scheduled to get back.

For a pilot's son, I didn't fly all that much.

But I had made the trip up to Mackinac and I had to say that it's one of my favorite places.

Some places are just good for the soul. And Mackinac Island is one of them.

A beautiful island at the top of the country. Horses and carriages. No cars. The only way to get to the island is by ferry or plane.

Knowing that and seeing the mansions along the edge of the lake and the Grand Hotel itself is just astounding. Not only is there a steady tourist industry during the summer, but a community of people who live there year round.

If I ever decided to give up the city life and move to a rural area, I would move to Mackinac Island.

That wasn't likely to happen. Houston was my home.

A second home wasn't out of the question though.

They returned right on time at dusk.

I watched the plane from a mere speck in the sky until they made a smooth landing and taxied over to the Skye Travels area.

I couldn't tell who was piloting the plane. If it was the applicant, she was probably getting the job.

Father was known to hire the best, though, so it wouldn't be surprising.

Darkness fell as they secured the plane. The full moon hung low in the sky, bright and big behind the city lights of downtown Houston.

The Houston skyline was rivaled only by the New York skyline.

Father stepped out of the plane first.

I caught myself holding my breath in anticipation of seeing the woman again.

But instead of the woman, a teenage girl stepped out and started across the tarmac.

Even from here, I could see the attitude exuding off her.

I should have checked the manifest, but I hadn't expected Father to be picking someone up.

Right on cue, I got a text from Momma.

MOMMA: *Are you still at the office?*

ME: *Yes.*

MOMMA: *Daddy is bringing Makenna home from Mackinac. I ordered some pizza for her. Will you make sure the delivery makes it? Daddy is interviewing someone.*

ME: *Sure.*

Mckenna was my half-sister Danielle's youngest child. Danielle's oldest daughter, Sarah, lived on Mackinac Island with her husband. Makenna visited her often.

The downside to working for the family business. After hours, especially, there was no one to delegate to.

I pulled my attention away from the plane.

I'd meet the woman later. If Father hired her. If he didn't, it didn't much matter anyway.

As I walked down the hallway to open the door for my niece, a clear and salient thought occurred to me.

It had been ten years.

Ten years.

It was time for me to let Noelle go.

They said if you love something set it free. If it was yours, it'll come back to you. If it wasn't yours, it won't.

Maybe I'd been holding onto something all these years that wasn't mine.

I ran a hand through my hair as I went down the elevator.

It was time.

Time for me to entertain the notion of dating someone else. All of my sisters were married or engaged. I didn't want to be the pathetic single uncle. Besides, I was tired of being lonely all the time.

As much as it hurt my heart, it was time to let Noelle go.

9

QUINN — BEFORE

One hundred business majors—college seniors—the cream of the crop—all together in one hotel at one time.

I didn't know what we were going to learn. Secrets of the top business people.

We were only allowed to know each other's first names. No last names allowed.

In fact, if anyone disclosed their last name, they were automatically expelled from the program.

No excused accepted.

There were, however, no rules against making friends. In fact, friends were encouraged.

It was just as well because if making friends was against the rules, I'd just go ahead and expel myself right now.

The girl sitting next to me was the most beautiful girl I had ever seen. Hands down.

She had delicate features. Big green eyes. Pink kissable lips. Long dark brunette hair that fell straight, but had little loose curls flipping at the ends.

She smelled fresh. Like spring flowers. Gardenia maybe.

I had four older sisters, so I was quite familiar with feminine scents. I was pretty sure it was her shampoo.

I had enough sense not to say anything.

"So we're not allowed to say where we're from either," I said, tapping the folder in front of her—I'd left my folder upstairs.

She shook her head.

"And don't even try to figure it out," she said. "because you'd never guess anyway."

"Now I'm intrigued," I said. I knew I'd try to figure it out even if it was against the rules. I wouldn't tell her, but I'd look for clues. I couldn't help myself.

"You're gonna get us both in trouble," she said.

I couldn't tell if the little drawl she added into that statement was natural or not. Her voice had a natural huskiness to it that was sexy as hell.

She had an accent I couldn't place. She was right though. I shouldn't even try.

After this program was over and we got our top secret certificate of completion, there would be nothing to stop us from disclosing personal information.

Unlike most people here, I already had a job.

I was going to be working for my family's company Skye Travels.

My father, a pilot, had started the company from nothing and it was my job to continue to grow it.

My father was good with business, but he didn't have a business degree. That's where I came in.

I wanted to make the company even better than it was. I wanted to grow it.

So when I'd been accepted into this elite training program I hadn't hesitated.

And now, if I hadn't believed in destiny before, I certainly did now.

If I hadn't come here I would never have met Noelle.

I knew nothing about her past… her future… her situation…

But in a few short minutes, I knew everything I needed to know about her.

Noelle was the girl I was going to marry.

10

NOELLE

Noah and I had spent the flight home discussing the terms of my employment.

Apparently my successful crosswind landing had impressed sufficiently enough that he wanted to hire me.

I hadn't expected a hands on interview like this, but it had turned out well.

The girl we'd picked up at the Mackinac airport sat behind us, music blaring in her ears, a surly expression on her face.

Noah told me she was his daughter's child, Makenna. His daughter with his first wife. Noah was prolific not only in business but also in children. He had a daughter by a first wife that he was now divorced from and five children with his college sweetheart whom he'd reconnected with after a number of years and married.

I don't know what the girl—his granddaughter was doing on Mackinac Island and it wasn't my business to ask.

It was my business to fly this airplane and get us home.

I could relax some now that I'd gotten the job.

I could… but I didn't.

Now I was flying for the boss.

He was going to pay for this flight.

But I didn't care about that. My retirement from the Air Force alone gave me enough money to live comfortably. I just wanted to work. To be productive.

I'd always worked and the thought of not having anything to do every day… to not having structure… was overwhelming.

After Noah and I ran out of things to discuss and sat quietly during the final descent, I allowed my thoughts some freedom. They ran in about a hundred different directions.

I'd gotten the job I wanted. In Houston.

Tomorrow I could start looking for an apartment.

Unless Noah wanted me to take a flight.

In which case, I'd be living in a hotel that much longer.

I didn't mind either way.

Actually, I was ready to start work.

Ready to get on with the next phase of my life.

I'd joined the Air Force running and hadn't stopped since.

While others were out drinking and partying while off-duty, I'd been studying.

I could fly just about any airplane, military or civilian.

I memorized airport codes. I studied flight manuals. I did everything I could to be the best.

Being a female in a man's world was challenging and I planned on standing above the crowd, man's world or not.

Besides, I'd met the one man I wanted to spend the rest of my life with.

The only problem was… I hadn't been able to find him.

I didn't know his last name or even where he was from or where he'd been headed. We'd met at a college program for elite business students.

Then I hadn't even stayed with business, but I'd learned a lot nonetheless.

I'd learned how to get ahead and it had paid off for me.

I'd retired as a Lie and a pilot.

Not something just anybody had been able to do.

I'd flown below the radar and kept my nose clean.

When early retirement came up, I'd taken it because I could read the tea leaves.

They asked nicely the first time.

The second time around they wouldn't be asking so nicely and the third time, they'd find a way to make it happen willingly or not.

At any rate, I'd missed out on the only man I ever really love simply because I'd stubbornly played by the rules even after the rules no longer applied.

I'd had a secondary motive.

I'd already made the commitment to join the military and I didn't know where that would take me.

I'd watched my mother follow my father around the country and even finally Germany.

She'd never really gotten to have a life. No friends. No steady job.

I couldn't do that to someone.

And I wasn't willing or even able to give up my military career.

Serving my country was in my genes.

I was going to do it come hell or high water.

Besides, I'd signed a contract, so it was out of my hands.

So I'd let him go.

His name was Quinn. That was all I knew.

I'd let him go.

But I'd never stopped loving him.

And I never would.

11

NOELLE —BEFORE

Quinn and I sat on the hotel roof—made into a cozy little patio, eating sandwiches for dinner.

It wasn't anything fancy. None of the meals were. But we didn't care.

We could have a taxi and gone to a real restaurant. Lots of nice places to eat in Houston, but we were content to stay here.

Seven days in to the fourteen-day program and we'd eaten every meal together.

The directors had been smart. They'd given the girls rooms in one wing of the hotel and the boys rooms in another.

The hotel was so big, we had to use different elevators to get to our rooms.

The late evening Houston air was balmy and perfect.

There was a high school not too far from here.

And it was Friday night. Football night.

Though we couldn't really see the game, we could hear it. We could hear snippets of the announcements and we could hear the band.

"I love this time of year," I said, taking a bite of my turkey sandwich.

"What do you love about it?" Quinn asked, leaning back on one elbow watching me. He watched me all the time, though he didn't think I knew it.

"Everything," I waved a hand encompassing it all. "The cool weather. The high school football game. The band playing."

"I like it, too," he said. "Were you in the band?"

"No." I hadn't been in one place long enough to be part of anything like that.

"A cheerleader then?" He turned up his bag of chips and dumped the last of the crumbs into his mouth.

"No," I said. Again, not anywhere long enough.

It was one of my regrets. I'd desperately wanted to be part of something. I wouldn't have cared if it was the band or a cheerleader. A majorette maybe.

But it had been out of my control. Part of the lifestyle of being an army brat.

No long lasting friendships and no time to become part of any sort of organized school group. It hadn't stopped me from trying it a couple of times, but we'd just moved after a few months and I had to start all over again.

"Why not?" he asked.

"I don't think I'm supposed to tell you that," I said. "It would give you clues about me."

"No one's listening," he said, his voice low, sending a shiver down my back.

I watched him, too, when he wasn't looking. He made it hard not to get close. We were close enough as it was.

"We've made it one week," I said, finishing off my sandwich. "Let's make the last one and get our certificates."

He shrugged. Again, despite his statements to the contrary, I got the feeling this program wasn't all that important to him.

This program was supposed to give us a leg up when we went to interview for jobs. It essentially guaranteed any potential employer that we had the training and skills needed to be in a managerial position, even though we might not have the experience yet.

But I wouldn't be interviewing, at least not for a really long time.

The day after graduation, I was leaving for active duty in the Air Force.

It was a decision I'd made over a year ago.

My parents had discouraged me from joining the military. They told me it was hard on relationships. And children.

I knew all that from firsthand experience.

I'd assured them in the cocky way only a college student could that I wasn't going to be getting married or have children.

And I had believed that with all my heart.

Until I met Quinn.

12

NOELLE

After we landed, Makenna, the surly teenager disappeared somewhere inside the building. The teenager did nothing to change my mind about not having children.

I left my options open and reserved the right to change my mind, but she wasn't making that happen today.

After securing the airplane, I followed Noah Worthington inside the Skye Travels building.

We rode up to the third floor and crossed the empty lobby. The receptionist desk was closed, the computer turned off, and the lights off.

Noah was probably used to being here after hours.

I caught a glimpse of the girl sitting in the break room, a box of pizza in front of her.

Good. She would be occupied for a few minutes at least.

I followed Noah into his spacious corner office. No clutter here.

Everything was put away, leaving a large oak desk with nothing but a computer sitting on it.

In the corner, in front of floor to ceiling windows, were two comfortable looking armchairs.

"Have a seat," he said. "I think my son is still here. He's the Vice-President and handles the contracts. We can start that tomorrow, but I'd like you to meet him."

"Sure," I said, taking a seat in one of the chairs. I took the moment alone to change back into my high heels. This still felt like part of the interview and I felt underdressed in my flats. Flats were fine for my uniform, but this outfit definitely called for heels.

From here, I had a perfect view of the tarmac, the downtown skyline, and the bright full moon hanging low in the early evening sky.

I'd lived a lot of places, most of them smaller towns where the Air Force bases were located, but I'd always had an affinity for the cities. And Houston was one of the prettiest skylines.

A few minutes later, I heard male voices out in the hallway.

I stood up, preferring to face my battles standing up. I don't know why this felt like a battle.

Probably because I hadn't interviewed for anything since... well... ever.

Noah walked in. He was strikingly handsome for a grandfather. Tall and lean. A full head of gray hair to be envied by men far younger than him.

It was some kind of law that men got better looking with age.

He stepped aside and another man, of similar height and build followed him inside.

I placed a hand on the arm of the chair and as my eyes snagged on the younger man.

Noah had said this was his son—the vice-president of Skye Travels.

The Vice-President would be a business major.

His blue eyes locked onto mine.

And something clicked in my memory.

It was a memory from long ago, but not buried.

His face was the first thing I thought about in the mornings and the last thing I thought about at night.

"Noelle," Noah said. "This is Quinn."

13

QUINN

As I stood in my father's office, a jet landed outside on the tarmac. Somewhere in the back of my mind, it registered that it wasn't one of ours. We had no other planes scheduled back here until sometime tomorrow.

My world narrowed down to just my father's corner office. He was rarely here anymore. Maybe three times a week. He and Momma were doing more and more things together.

They'd made their fortune, raised their family, and were enjoying their time together.

Not retired. Neither of them would ever retire. They loved what they did too much.

My father had just hired a new pilot.

The woman he'd had fly him to Mackinac Island and back.

She wasn't just any pilot. And she wasn't just any woman.

She was Noelle Winston.

The woman I'd been searching for.

For ten years.

A handful of minutes ago, I'd stood in the elevator and vowed to myself to set her free.

To move on.

Even though it was no more than what should have been a simple mental decision, it had broken my heart to do it.

Maybe ten years was long enough to wait for someone I'd only spent two weeks with.

Maybe the whole letting go thing worked.

Maybe I should have let go of Noelle years ago.

She was standing right here in front of me... looking at me the same way I was looking at her.

As though the world had just flipped over on its axis.

The irony of it all was astounding. The girl I'd seen on the tarmac earlier—the one my father was interviewing—had prompted this decision. That inkling of interest I'd felt for the mystery girl had been up front and in my face that I wasn't being rational.

And that very mystery woman was Noelle.

Neither one of us said anything.

Father walked to his desk. Unlocked his computer screen, then looked over at us. It took a minute for the situation to register with him.

"You two know each other?" he asked.

"Yes."

"We've met."

"Well," he said, looking from one of us to the other and back again. "I'll just go check on the girl."

"Noelle," I said.

"Quinn." She closed the distance between us and wrapped her arms around my waist in a hug.

It took a second for my stunned brain to react and by the time it did, she'd stepped back.

Her voice had that sexy huskiness that had I'd heard in my dreams night after night.

I recovered enough to grab her hands.

Keeping her there in front of me, I looked into her eyes. They were as green as I remembered.

I soaked in her features. The curve of her jaw. Her dark, thick eyelashes framing those clear green eyes. Her perfect bow-shaped lips, begging to be kissed.

But ten years was too long.

Too many years had passed for me to follow my instinct and pull her into a kiss.

But damn, that instinct was strong.

How many times had I dreamed about seeing her again?

How many different ways had I imagined running into her again?

A thousand different ways.

I'd even imagined her walking into the Skye Travels terminal to take a flight.

As a passenger.

Never once had I imagined her standing here in my father's office. My father's latest new hire. A pilot.

The Noelle I knew was a business major. Like me.

What strange turn of events had occurred to get us to this moment?

Nearly ten years to the day.

14

NOELLE

I hadn't looked for Quinn.

Not really.

I may have typed his name into a google search a couple of times. I might even have looked for people named Quinn on Facebook.

But Quinn and business had yielded nothing but pages and pages of strangers. I didn't even know where he was from.

Besides, what would I do if I did happen across him? It would have only hurt me to see that he'd moved on with his life. As he should have.

I was the one who had insisted that we not disclose our last names.

I kept thinking that I couldn't do that to him.

He would have wanted to stay together and I was entering a way of life that I couldn't in all fairness subject him to.

Any future we would have had wouldn't have been fair to him.

Quinn had been one of the top business students in the country at the same time I was.

My gaze flicked down to our hands. To his left hand.

There was no ring on his left hand.

That didn't mean anything.

I tried to steady my heart rate. I felt like I was coming out of an aileron roll.

"How are you here?" I asked.

A slow grin spread across his face.

"I think that's the question I should be asking you," he said. "You're a pilot?"

I nodded.

"How is that possible?" he asked.

I shrugged. "Air Force."

He looked at me sideways.

"Wait a minute," he said, pulling me with him to sit across from him in the chair I'd just vacated.

He sat forward, not letting go of my hands, searching my eyes.

It was as though if he let go of me I would disappear.

"Before," he said. "Ten years ago. Were you Air Force?"

"I was ROTC," I said. "so yes."

"Then… why?"

I knew what he was asking.

He wanted to know why I wouldn't tell him who I was. How to stay in touch with me.

"Because," I said, looking toward the window. Toward the Houston skyline and the majestic full moon behind it.

He'd been here in Houston all along.

We'd met in Houston and he could have been from anywhere. But he'd been from here all along. I could have figured it out if I'd tried. Or if I'd let him, he would have told me.

He wanted to tell me.

He had told me. But I hadn't wanted to know.

Because if I knew if I'd known I wouldn't have been able to stay away from him.

15

NOELLE — BEFORE

He was waiting for me next to the water fountain where he waited for me every morning.

The water fountain was in the middle of the hotel, separating the two towers. His room was in one and mine was in the other.

The fountain itself was three stories high, the water splashing loudly as it fell against the rectangular pool with concrete benches along the edges.

Today was the day.

We'd received our certificates last night. Out of one hundred people, we were only two of the ten who had successfully completed the training.

My lips were still swollen from our time together last night.

But now it was time for us to say goodbye.

My heart was heavy as I walked toward him.

He took my hands and looked into my eyes.

"I don't want to say goodbye," he said.

"Neither do I," I said.

And I was afraid that if I stayed here with him, his hands

holding onto mine like a lifeline, that I would try to find a way to do just that.

To upend my life to be with him.

But I'd signed my contract. I'd sealed my fate.

There was no turning back for me now.

And I could not—would not—subject him to a military lifestyle. He would get a good job. A great job. Probably the CEO of a company somewhere. He'd make millions. He'd have a good life.

I would only bring him down. A man couldn't move up the corporate ladder while following his wife around the country.

My mother had drilled that into my head for as long as I could remember.

The military life was not designed for families.

As much as she loved my father, she made it clear that she regretted living her life moving from place to place.

She wouldn't get that time back.

Like my father, I'd made my choice, but unlike my father, I wouldn't bring anyone with me.

Especially not Quinn. I cared too deeply for him.

I had to let him go.

"Is there anything I can do to change your mind?" he asked.

I shook my head, realizing too late that tears streamed down my cheeks.

I bit my bottom lip. My heart was aching.

If I didn't go now, I wasn't going to be able to do this.

"I have to go," I said, looking down at our hands. "I have to catch my flight."

"Let me ride with you to the airport," he said.

I shook my head.

"I can't," I said passed the lump in my throat.

"Just a little more time," he said.

A little more time would tear me apart.

"We decided," I said.

"No, my love," he said, causing a hitch in my breath. "You decided."

As I pulled my hands out of his, I looked into his face, memorizing every feature. Knowing I would never see him again.

But he'd made an indelible mark on my heart.

Before I turned away, he pressed a folded slip of paper into my palm.

"What's this?" I asked.

"When…if… you change your mind," he said. "This number will always reach me. No matter how long you wait."

I shook my head, but my fingers closed around the little slip of paper.

"Let's not say goodbye," he said. "I'll see you around."

"You're a cowboy now," I said, teasing him about an earlier conversation.

"Well," he drawled. "this is Houston, Texas."

"Yes," I said. "It is."

And I really did have a plane to catch.

"I'll see you around," I said.

Then I turned and walked to the front door of the hotel.

My hand on the door, I turned and looked over my shoulder.

He was watching me. And it broke my heart.

There was no turning back now.

Blindly, I walked down the sidewalk toward one of the waiting yellow taxis.

I passed a large wastebasket on my way.

As I passed, I dropped the slip of paper into that wastebasket.

Then I opened the door and slid into the back seat of the taxi.

16

QUINN

"Because why?" I persisted.

There was so much I didn't understand. So much I needed to understand.

Father and my niece were down the hall talking.

Probably sharing the pizza that had been delivered earlier.

It was odd to hear my niece actually having a conversation. She'd been a sweet child who had somehow grown into a surly teen, but my father had a way of connecting with people.

I couldn't let go of Noelle's hands. The last time I had let her go, it had taken years for her to walk back into my life.

"I knew I was going into the Air Force," she said. "I knew what the military life was like." She paused and took a breath.

"You were raised in a military family?"

"My father," she said. "A retired full bird colonel."

I looked away, toward the window at the blackness outside. That explained so much.

"I see."

"My mother hated it. She told me it's no life for a family."

She stopped abruptly and bit her bottom lip.

Something she'd never stopped doing.

"So do you have one?" I asked. "A family?"

I needed to know now. Right now. Before I lost the nerve to ask.

I didn't want to know it if she did, but I needed to know. I needed to know which way to go.

I didn't know what I was going to do if she already had a family.

"No," she whispered. "No family."

I slowly let out the breath I'd been holding.

Then I brought one of her hands to my lips and kissed the back of her fingers.

"Tell me, Noelle," I said. "Did you call the number I gave you?"

It was the only explanation I could think of. I'd given her the phone number for Skye Travels. It was a number I was confident would never change. My cell phone number could change, but not that one.

Maybe she'd called it and decided to become a pilot.

"No," she said. "I never looked at it."

"You didn't open it?"

She shook her head.

"I didn't keep it," she said. "If I had…"

"You wanted to make sure you weren't tempted."

She nodded. "I'm sorry."

"It's okay," I said. "You did what you thought was best."

I wasn't mad at her. I was far too happy to see her.

"What about you?" she asked. "This is your company?"

"My father's."

I couldn't stop looking at her. This girl had disappeared off the face of the earth, but somehow she'd ended up right here.

"And your family?" she asked, glancing at my hand again. It was the second time she'd done that.

"I'm not married," I said.

She was looking out the window again.

"Were you?" she asked, looking back at me.

"Was I married? No."

"How is that so?" she asked, turning back to me.

"I never met anyone else like you," I said, though it wasn't completely the truth. The truth was that I had waited for her.

But I didn't know if I should tell her that. It had been ten years after all.

That was an inordinate amount of time to wait for someone a man may or may not ever see again.

Noelle slipped her hands out of mine as we heard Father's footsteps coming down the hallway.

He stood in the doorway and looked inside.

"I'm gonna head out," he said. "We can finish up the paperwork tomorrow."

"Of course," Noelle said, standing up. "I should be going, too.

"I'll give you a ride," I said.

She just thought she was going to get away from me that easily this time.

I had ten years of catching up to do.

17

NOELLE

There were rules. There were always rules.

And I didn't know the Skye Travels rules yet.

It was best not to start breaking rules before you even knew what they were.

In the military culture I'd come from, dating a superior or in this case a supervisor or member of management was trouble.

I wasn't even on the payroll yet. Not officially.

But Quinn was being persistent.

Noah and the teenage girl walked ahead of us down the hallway.

Quinn ducked into what was no doubt his office for about two seconds, I grabbed my suitcase, then we all waited while he turned off the lights.

To his credit, Noah didn't say anything while we waited for the elevator.

I kept my chin up and my gaze straight ahead.

I'd been well-trained on keeping my composure during uncomfortable situations. When in doubt, say nothing.

So I said nothing.

While we rode the elevator down, Quinn watched me.

I couldn't help but wonder what he thought.

I worked for him now... for his father anyway. What, exactly did Quinn think would happen?

I tried to put things in perspective. To see things the way he might. We'd essentially had a college romance. A short, but intense one. Like a summer romance, except it hadn't been summer. And it had been shorter.

A lot of time had passed. We'd had different experiences.

We couldn't just pick up where we'd left off.

That didn't happen.

Not after ten years.

Besides, Quinn wasn't telling his father about me.

That was never a good sign.

I wasn't interested in a fling for old time's sake.

Not with Quinn.

He'd meant too much to me for that.

After we reached the bottom floor and Noah and the teenager walked toward Noah's car, I slowed and pulled out my phone.

"I can call an Uber," I said.

"Why would you do that?" Quinn asked, looking at me like I'd lost my mind.

"I don't want to be a bother and my hotel is in the other direction."

I don't know why I said that. I had no idea which way Quinn was headed. Had no way of knowing.

"That's odd," Quinn said. "because I wasn't headed in any particular direction. Across the street maybe for a drink."

"Right," I said, tucking my phone back into my handbag.

"Come on," he said, taking my suitcase. "Let's have a drink."

Since I couldn't figure out a graceful way to get out of it, I followed him and slid into the passenger side of his BMW sedan.

Besides, if I was truthful with myself, I wanted to have a drink with Quinn.

Quinn Worthington.

Who would have thought?

18

QUINN

We found a booth toward the back of the Skyhouse Bar across the street.

The Skyhouse was a modern building strategically placed across the highway from the private terminal side of the airport.

It had a mixture of booths and tables and an ample number of barstools in front of the long marble bar. The lights were low, the music uplifting.

The Skyhouse Bar, no relation to Skye Travels, much to my chagrin, was a regular hangout for private pilots.

They not only had good food, but they had the best martinis. Of course pilots tended to come more for the food than the drinks.

The evenings were a different story. The Skyhouse attracted locals coming in for the martinis. Tonight was no different. In fact, it was fairly crowded. We were lucky to find a seat at all.

Indiscernible eighties music provided a background for conversation and laughter.

Noelle slid into one side of the booth and I sat across

from her.

I couldn't stop looking at her and marveling that she was really here.

I'd searched everywhere for her and she just waltzed into my father's office like it's no big deal at all.

The server, a college student named Megan stopped at our booth.

"The usual?" she asked me.

I nodded.

"And for the lady?"

"I'll have the same," she said.

I smiled. Noelle didn't know what the usual was. It was a brave move to blindly order what I ordered.

"Good deal. Be right back," Megan said and bounced through the crowd.

"A pilot," I said, steepling my fingers and looking into her eyes. "How did that happen?"

Pressing her hands against the edge of the table, she leaned back.

"I scored high on the test," she said with a little shrug.

"But you score high on all tests," I said, thinking of the two-week program where we'd met.

"I know," she said. "But at the time, I wasn't too interested in pursuing business."

"Why not?" I asked, wondering if she was burned out from the program we'd gone through.

Megan brought our drinks and set them on the table in front of us.

"Here you go," she said. "Can I get you anything to eat?"

I looked questioningly at Noelle.

"Not now," she said.

Megan bounced away, leaving us alone, cocooned in a little bubble, surrounded by the noise and activity around us.

"You were here all along?" she asked.

"All along."

"So you're from here?"

I nodded.

"I should have known that." She took a sip of her drink.

"You really didn't call the number?" I asked.

If she'd called the number she would have known. How had she not called the number?

"I really didn't," she said with a little smile.

It was starting to sink in a little bit that she was really here.

I was having random thoughts. Like... We could start dating.

My phone chimed with a text message.

I slid it out of my pocket.

FATHER: *Is Noelle with you?*

ME: *Yes.*

FATHER: *She isn't answering her texts.*

"My father is texting you," I said.

"How do you know?" she asked, reaching for her handbag.

I held up my phone.

"I have to go," she said, looking up at me with a perplexed expression.

"What's wrong?"

She slid her martini glass, barely touched, toward the middle of the table.

"He wants me to take a flight," she said. "A passenger to Dallas. Tomorrow."

"Welcome to Skye Travels."

She sent a quick text back to Noah confirming that she'd be there and looked over at me.

"I should get some sleep," she said.

And just like that she was walking away from me again.

19

NOELLE

Sitting in the car with Quinn at the wheel was a bit surreal.

The car still had that new car smell. Personally I'd never owned a new car. Since most of my time was spent on base, it didn't make a lot of sense to spend money on something I'd rarely use for more than driving the couple of miles to the office and home again.

The two weeks I'd spent with Quinn ten years ago had been spent mostly in a hotel. We'd only gone out one time and then we'd ridden in the back seat of a taxi.

He maneuvered the Houston traffic smoothly as we headed toward uptown where I'd reserved a hotel.

It actually made no sense for me to spend the night in uptown because it was a fairly long drive from the airport. But it was the area I was somewhat familiar with and the area where I would probably look for an apartment. So all in all, I was thinking ahead.

It was a bit fortuitous, though, because it was in the general direction Quinn lived.

"Are you sure this isn't out of your way?" I asked.

"Noelle," he said. "I promise it's not, but even if you needed to go in the completely opposite direction, I'd still drive you."

A warmth spread through me that reminded me of how close we'd gotten during a short time ten years ago. I'd have to think about this later. It was too much for me to consider with him sitting right beside me.

"You have a house?" I asked.

"A condo," he said.

Of course. A condo suited him.

The unmarried Vice-President of a successful Houston company wouldn't need a house. He would live in a condo, something that didn't require a lot of yard maintenance.

"Are you still in the Air Force?" he asked.

"They call it early retirement," I said. Retirement was a word I hated. It made me think of older people who had no ambition left in life.

I was so far from that. I was just getting started.

To his credit, Quinn didn't comment.

"Why Houston?" he asked.

Why Houston, indeed.

I wasn't going to tell him that my fondest memories were from those two weeks I'd spent with him in Houston. It wasn't that I'd had a bad childhood or teenage years. It was just… well… he was Quinn.

I looked out the window as we exited off the freeway and headed toward my hotel. High rise buildings stretched toward the sky on both sides of us.

"I've heard good things about Skye Travels," I said. It wasn't a lie. I had heard good things about the company. I'd just gone about my job search a bit backwards. I'd picked the city first.

I was having trouble wrapping my head around going to work for Quinn's company.

That he had lived in Houston all along and I hadn't known it.

He would have been so easy to find if I'd only let myself do it.

I straightened in my chair and lifted my chin.

Now was not the time for regrets.

I'd done what I thought was right.

I'd sacrificed a life with Quinn to protect him.

I hadn't been able to change my own life course, but I didn't have to bring Quinn into it with me.

It had been simpler that way.

We pulled up in front of my hotel and Quinn waved off the valet.

The motor idled quietly and air blew lightly from the vents.

Soft moonlight streamed through the open sunroof, barely competing with the bright streetlights.

"Where are you living now?" he asked.

I shrugged and looked over at him out of the corner of my eyes.

"Define living."

He looked at me strangely.

"I guess it's where your stuff is," he said.

I put a hand against my brow.

"Then I guess I'm living in your trunk."

20

QUINN

Surely I hadn't heard her right.

Was Noelle saying that she was homeless?

I had to wave off the valet again, a different guy this time. This was an upscale hotel. Not the kind of place a homeless person would spend the night.

"I think I have misunderstood you," I said.

"I don't think so. I put everything in storage and brought what I need."

I unbuckled my seatbelt and turned in my seat to face her.

I had just bought this car two weeks ago and I had to say that Noelle looked good in it. She would have looked good in anything, but she most definitely looked good in this car.

"I have four sisters," I said. "Five if you count my half-sister. Not a single one of them, not even my sister Ainsley who is a pilot, could put everything she needed to live off of for more than one night in that little suitcase."

"You forget," she said. "I'm a military girl. And..." she picked up the oversized handbag from the floor in front of her. "this is my overnight bag."

"That's kind of impressive," I said. And a little bit disconcerting. I was accustomed to girls like my sisters. Girls who had lots of clothes and who traveled anything but light. Not girls like Noelle who could put all their essential belongings in one bag and everything else in storage. I wasn't sure I knew how to relate to someone who could survive on less than I could.

"Car?" he asked.

"Sold it before I left Spokane."

"So you're going to be doing some shopping," I said.

She was going to need a car, an apartment, and personal items.

"What time's your flight in the morning?" I asked, glancing at the time. It was just after eight.

"Nine thirty," she said.

"I'll pick you up on the way to the office in the morning," I said.

"I'll be ready."

She didn't even ask what time. That was twice she'd done that now. First when we'd ordered drinks. And now.

"You can check out in the morning, too."

"Am I changing hotels?" she asked with a little smile.

I shook my head.

"You don't need to stay in a hotel," I said. "when I have a perfectly good guest room."

"I can't do that," she said.

"Why not?" I asked.

"Nepotism."

I laughed. "I work for my father. Can't get much more nepotistic."

She smiled then and looked right at me.

That probably wasn't the best thing she could have done.

I wanted to kiss her. Right here. Right now.

Everything around us faded.

The lights from the hotel. The sounds from the cars on the street.

Everything.

And the ten years that had passed since that last night we'd spent together faded away, too.

All this time.

And all I'd had to do was to let her go.

21

NOELLE — BEFORE

I stood next to Quinn on the escalator behind the tall three-story water fountain in the middle of the hotel.

The fountain was lit with sparkly clear lights, glowing behind the water.

Soft music drifted from one of the two hotel bars. We hadn't been to either of them. The program directors had successfully filled far too many hours during the past two weeks.

Now that I'd done this, officer training camp was going to be a walk in the park.

I held my plaque up next to the identical one Quinn was holding.

They were exactly the same except for our names.

We'd done it. Two of the ten people out of one hundred.

Three of the other ten were a few feet behind us, laughing and talking. Two guys and a girl who'd formed close friendships just as Quinn and I had.

"I guess we don't have to worry about anybody monitoring our activities anymore," Quinn said.

I looked over my shoulder. I didn't see any of our instructors. Just the three students and a couple of strangers.

I agreed with him, since we'd been specifically told that we were free to go. Of course, it was already seven o'clock, so no one was going too far tonight.

"I don't know," I said. "I think it's best if we play it safe."

He looked at me sideways as we reached the bottom floor and stepped off the escalator. I'd been the one to insist that we play by the rules the whole time. Quinn had been ready for us to disclose our last names from the first day.

"Okay," he said. "we'll do it your way."

I wouldn't say it was my way exactly. I had a reason beyond completing this program.

Tomorrow I was catching a plane to Montgomery, Alabama for officer training school.

I'd already decided not to tell Quinn.

I suspected he liked me enough to try to take our relationship to the next level and I knew I was. But I was fighting it every step of the way.

Not a good idea. I told myself that every time I looked at Quinn's handsome, strong jawline, sparkling blue eyes, and lips that begged to be kissed.

There had been no touching and certainly no kissing. That reality did nothing to keep the thoughts at bay. If wishes could be kisses... oh my.

Then I would sternly remind myself that my life was going to be chaotic. I could be moving as often as every three years. And I'd signed up for a twenty-year career of it. twenty years was a lifetime. I'd be an ancient forty-two when I could retire. Not that I would want to. Retirement, in my book, was a kiss of death. I had far too much energy and ambition. I'd find a way to combine my business degree with my military training. That was my goal anyway.

At any rate, the military life in my future was no life for a man like him—a man with unlimited potential in life.

"Let's at least leave this hotel and go celebrate," he said. His hand bumped mine as we walked. We'd been walking side by side for two weeks. That had never happened. It sent a spark of awareness all the way through me.

I might have thought it was intentional, except that he was looking straight ahead.

Then he looked over at me with a sideways grin that sent my heart rate into overdrive.

"Come on," he said. "Let's grab a taxi and go get a drink."

I already knew it was almost impossible for me to refuse him.

Quinn was trouble.

Trouble.

22

NOELLE

Quinn had my thoughts shooting in about ten different directions.

My defenses were down. It wasn't the long day. I was used to long days. A commercial flight from Spokane to Houston. Then I'd flown to Mackinac Island and back. Been offered a new job on the spot.

And then I'd been reunited with the love of my life. Whether I admitted it or not, that's what he was.

Okay. Maybe it was the long day.

If not physical fatigue, then definitely emotional.

When I woke up this morning, I had expected to simply fly to Houston, have a quick interview, then go to my hotel room and regroup.

Today was the first day of my brand-new life. I'd expected a lifetime of being in the military. Instead I was unexpectedly out. A veteran. A civilian.

I'd expected to have a job based on my business degree. Instead, I'd completely changed directions and now I was a pilot.

I couldn't really explain why I'd made that leap. I think it had been unexpected, first of all, and second, my head was still reeling from leaving Quinn.

I had a clear memory of my heavy heart. I so wanted to go with him wherever he was going. He hadn't asked me to, though, and although I wished that he had, I knew it was good that he hadn't.

I'd dated some. I'd even had a boyfriend for three years. A civilian banker. He'd liked me, I think, because I spoke his business language. Then I'd gotten transferred.

I was secretly relieved, though I'd never told anyone. It had been a comfortable relationship. One that I had been content with.

I'd expected to have to settle for someone I loved. Not the one man I was in love with. But today, I'd been reunited with the man who had stolen my heart all those years ago.

"Penny for your thoughts," Quinn said.

I chuckled and looked out at the hotel entrance. A doorman stood like a guard at attention—waiting for the next person to come in or out. Not something I expected to see at a hotel.

"Just how odd all this is," I said. "How unexpected."

Quinn took a deep breath and turned his air conditioning vent away from his face.

"I imagined how we might find each other," he said. "but I never once thought you'd show up at Skye Travels." He put one hand on the back of my seat. "As a pilot."

"Me either," I said.

"Did you know?" he asked. "Did you already know that you were going to be a pilot... back then?"

I adjusted the handbag at my feet. Slipped my right foot out of its shoe for just a moment of relief from the tight uncomfortable leather.

"Not a clue," I said. "I knew I was going into the Air Force as an officer. I thought that my degree would be useful."

"Was it?" he asked.

Was it? I often wondered.

"I'm sure it was," I said. "They say knowledge is power. Right?"

"That's what they say."

He tapped his fingertips on the steering wheel with his left hand.

"Noelle," he said. "I 'um…"

I held my breath. I didn't know what I wanted him to say. There were so many things unsaid between us.

If I could go back… if I could turn back the hands of time, I would have chosen him. I would have taken that risk. There was no way to know which direction we would go.

But I'd been young and dumb. I'd chosen the job over the man.

I wouldn't do that again.

Unfortunately, it could be too late. Was it too late?

I bit my bottom lip as I waited for him to finish his sentence.

"I'm happy to see you," he said.

23

QUINN

It wasn't what I'd been thinking.

I couldn't tell her what I'd been thinking.

I waited for you.

It had been ten years.

Ten years.

No man in his right mind would wait for a girl for ten years. Not a girl he didn't know how to find.

And we'd only had two weeks together. No doubt I would be ridiculed by both men and women alike. Even though I kept myself out of such situations, I'd still been propositioned more times than I could remember.

I'd made a promise, but Noelle hadn't.

By all rights, she shouldn't be here.

The first valet came up to my door again. I tapped the button and the window slowly lowered.

"Sir," he said. "Can I park your car? Or would you like to park over there?" He pointed to a self-parking area off to the left.

"I'm just dropping off," I said. There was no one behind us. The guy was just being impatient.

I glanced at the clock. Had we really been sitting here for twenty minutes?

"I'll just be a minute," I said.

"Thank you," the valet said, turning and walking back toward the front of the hotel.

"I think they want us to move," I said, turning back to Noelle.

She was looking at me with hooded eyes. And for just a moment I saw a deep sadness. Then she smiled and I decided I had imagined it.

"I'll go," she said. "It's been a long day."

"I'll get your luggage." As I opened the door, the cool evening breeze slapped me in the face, jarring me out of the trance I'd been in.

I closed the door and popped the trunk.

I pulled Noelle's suitcase out of the trunk and set it on the ground.

Just a few hours and I'd pick her up again.

But I didn't want to leave her. Not even for those few hours.

My love had not dimmed. It had merely been banked… waiting… simmering below the surface.

I opened my arms and she walked into them. I took heart that she didn't hesitate.

Then as she wrapped her arms around my waist and rested her cheek against my chest, her head just under my chin, everything except the soft feel of her faded.

Her hair smelled like gardenia. Just like it had so very long ago.

We stood that way as the seconds passed and I would have stood that way forever.

"The valet is gonna come back and ask us to move again," she whispered, shifted her head just enough to remind me that we couldn't actually stay this way forever, no matter how much I wanted to.

"You're right," I said. "I'll see you in the morning. And don't forget to check out. Your room is already ready.

Once I got her home with me, I would stand a better chance of keeping her.

And that, I decided, was just what I was going to do.

24

NOELLE

My trip to Dallas had been a quick drop off. The passenger was a pleasant business man—a self-made millionaire who had started his own waste sorting service out of nothing.

He invented a machine that sorts ordinary trash into categories that could be recycled and sold from biodegradable trash for the landfills. So instead of competing with existing companies, he jumped right in the middle of them and created a brand-new process.

Now that he had established his company in Houston, he was talking to investors in Dallas to get his company established there, too.

If I had extra money lying around, I would have invested in it myself.

It was a brilliant idea.

Someone, maybe me, would have to fly back to Dallas to pick him up in a couple of days.

I had a visual on the Houston runway now and with it my heart rate shot into overdrive.

My blood raced as I thought about Quinn being there at the Skye Travels office.

He could look out his window and watch me land if he wanted to.

I normally didn't worry about who was watching me. I was a good pilot and I knew it. Anyone who'd been through the rigorous training I'd been through had no choice but to be good.

But knowing that Quinn could very possibly be watching made me want to make the best landing I could.

I wanted him to be proud of me. Perhaps even a bit impressed.

When he'd picked me up that morning, he'd brought me a latte just the way I liked it.

Apparently, the way I took my coffee was one of those things that didn't change over the years.

I'd done as he asked. I'd checked out of the hotel. My luggage was actually in the trunk of his car right now.

There was something surprisingly intimate about that. It was almost like we were a couple.

We weren't, of course.

We hadn't seen each other for ten years.

People didn't just pick up like that without a hitch. Did they?

My landing gear was down. Flaps extended and spoilers activated.

This was one of my favorite parts of flying. That time when I was just above the treetops. When ground effect worked its magic to make the plane feel like it was floating above the ground.

Final permission to land came from traffic control.

My thoughts had been full of Quinn all day.

Even now, I had to push those thoughts aside and focus on what I was doing.

Nonetheless, my wheels touched down in a smooth as silk landing and then I taxied over to the private tarmac of Skye Travels.

I made my final checks, then opened the door.

There was no one waiting for me, of course. I wasn't expecting anyone to be.

But I had to admit, at least to myself, that I was a tad bit disappointed that Quinn wasn't here to meet me.

Geez. I had it bad.

A bad crush on the man who'd stolen my heart ten years ago.

25

NOELLE — BEFORE

Quinn held out a hand to help me out of the backseat of the taxi. His hand was strong and comforting.

We'd only gone about three blocks to a little place called The Big Easy.

Big band jazzy music spilled out the front doors along with a line.

"Looks like a popular place," I said. "How did you find it?"

"Somebody told me about it," he said vaguely.

As we walked across the parking lot and got in line, he kept his firm hold on my hand.

It was enough to distract me from worrying about who might have told him about his place.

The line was moving fast and we reached a window with a girl seated behind the glass.

"Two," Quinn said and I caught a glimpse of the black credit card he slid her way.

She slid two tickets our way and we walked toward the door to the next entry point.

"Do you want some money?" I asked as we waited. I asked

even though I had no idea what it cost. I wasn't sure he did either.

"The guy always pays," he said. "always."

Maybe in his world. In the world I came from girls were just as likely to pay as guys were.

A burly man stamped the back of our hands, leaving us branded with a little round striped symbol in black ink.

We stepped inside the building. There were people of all ages, mostly middle-aged people, filling the space. Sitting at tables, at the bar, and others were standing. I caught a glimpse of some pool tables in the back.

We found two empty stools together and slid onto them at the bar.

One of the two bartender—who looked insanely busy—looked over at Quinn. He held up two fingers.

The bartender set two bottles of beer in front of Quinn.

"How did he know?" I asked.

"How did he know what?" he asked, sliding a beer over in front of me.

I wasn't much of a beer person. In fact, I rarely drank alcohol at all, but the occasion seemed to warrant a change of pace.

"It's what they're known for," Quinn said.

And apparently he was right. Everyone sitting at the bar had a beer in front of them.

I shrugged it off. We were probably lucky to get service at all. Ordering something different would just take longer.

I took a sip of the beer. Thankfully it was in a bottle. Otherwise I wouldn't have been able to drink it. At least in a bottle, the smell was less noticeable.

In a belated toast, Quinn held up his bottle.

"To two weeks," he said.

I didn't say anything. Just tapped my bottle lightly against his.

Two weeks was a rather vague statement.

He could have said *Two weeks of hell.* Or *Two weeks of friendship.* Or *Two weeks completed.*

"When do you leave?" he asked, looking at me with hooded eyes.

"In the morning." I had a flight out to Alabama. I'd had the ticket for two months.

Right now I was wishing I didn't.

But wishes were like snowflakes. Beautiful and fleeting.

Just like friendships.

This moving around from place to place thing was the very reason I avoided getting too close to anyone.

But these two weeks, I'd let my guard down. I'd let my pretend to be normal. Pretend that I could have a normal relationship with someone.

It was a fantasy.

"Penny for your thoughts," Quinn said, leaning forward so I could hear him.

I took a sip of beer, hiding my reaction.

I couldn't tell him that I was thinking about how it would be to have a normal relationship with him... or a relationship at all.

We'd been nothing but friends. Sure, I could see him looking at me with what could only be called longing. And sure, he'd held my hand as we walked into a crowded bar.

No matter, I was flying out in the morning and the odds of ever seeing him again were too astronomically impossible to compute.

But... maybe this was my opportunity to take that fantasy to the next level.

Did I dare?

26

QUINN

I watched Noelle make a perfect landing. My veteran pilot father couldn't have done it any better. In fact, if I hadn't known that Noelle was the pilot in this particular landing, I might have thought it was my father.

Of course, when she stepped out of the plane onto the tarmac, any uncertainty dissipated.

She was wearing black slacks and a white button-down shirt. Her long hair was pulled back into a messy ponytail. No cap.

Jan would have to order her uniforms. Father insisted that all his pilots—male and female—wear caps. I agreed with Father that the caps set our pilots apart. Made our pilots look quintessentially professional.

Right now Noelle didn't need a cap to set her apart from anybody. She was both beautiful and professional looking.

And seeing her walking across the tarmac toward my office was one of my fantasies come true.

But I had never once imagined her walking across as a pilot. Passing through as a passenger, sure. But never working here.

Father knocked on my door, interrupting the fantasies

playing in my head at seeing her walk across the tarmac, the light breeze blowing her long hair behind her.

"Can we sit?" Father asked, going to sit at one of the two armchairs in the righthand corner of my office.

"Sure," I said, not sure why he asked since he was already sitting down.

"Your sister is flying in this afternoon," he said.

I knew he meant Madison, my oldest sister. That meant she'd be bringing her baby—the first grandchild. Not counting my half-sister, Danielle, of course, who already had five children of her own. Danielle lived in California and we rarely saw her or her children.

Besides, Madison's baby was Momma's first grandchild, so she was on track to be about as spoiled as they came. I certainly was doing my part. I had a rocking horse I'd ordered sitting in my condo waiting for her first birthday.

"Sunday dinner?" I asked.

"No doubt," Father said. "Might be nice enough for us all to be outside."

"I'll be there," I said.

Father nodded. Family dinners at the Worthington's weren't exactly optional.

"Bring Noelle," he said.

"Okay," I said, nearly losing my balance as I sat down in the chair next to him.

Needless to say, I was shocked by the request. I wouldn't have been surprised if Father had invited her, but he'd never asked me to do the inviting. It was something he always did himself.

I wanted to get this conversation over with. Noelle would be coming up to the offices and I wanted to see her. To talk to her.

"Is she the one?" Father asked, balancing a bottle of water on his knees.

"What do you mean?" This question was even more unsettling than him asking me to invite her.

"The one you met at the business program?" Father asked. "What was it? Ten years ago?"

Father was the only one I'd told about Noelle. And even then I'd been vague about it, not giving him any details.

I'd told him enough to make him leave me alone about dating. I'd told him in no uncertain terms that I was going to be waiting for her.

Apparently he'd taken me at my word. We'd never talked about it again and he'd never once asked me about dating anyone.

Neither him nor mother.

My sisters didn't know. I was pretty sure they just chalked it up to me being strange.

It was bad enough growing up the only brother with four sisters.

"So," Father asked. "Is she?"

It was clear to me that Father wasn't going to let me go without an answer.

"Yes," I said, feeling a lump in my throat at the admission. It was strange to talk about something I'd kept to myself for all these years.

And admitting to my father that Noelle was the woman I'd been waiting for these past years took more bravery than I ever thought it would.

27

NOELLE

I sat in what was a shared office space for Skye Travels pilots. It had two desks, one on the west wall and one on the east. Two chairs and one computer at each desk.

A huge abstract painting of a small jet, a Phenom 300, decorated the other wall.

Jan, who obviously took care of a myriad of details around the Skye Travels office, had taken my measurements and ordered my uniforms, then she'd shown me back here.

"Just wait here," she'd said. Jan was efficient. I got that. But she wasn't the friendliest person I'd ever met.

I tapped the computer keys and a background image came up. The Skye Travels logo.

I was getting the impression that Skye Travels was a bigger deal than I'd thought.

Wondering where Quinn was, I watched the door. But I seemed to be the only person around.

Hearing an incoming jet, I went to the window and watched the private plane land, then taxi over to this area.

This one had no logo, so obviously it wasn't one of Noah Worthington's fleet.

After the pilot and a middle-aged couple disembarked, they walked to the building next door. A few minutes later, a technician taxied the airplane over to one of the other hangars.

I was about to go find Jan to see what I was supposed to be doing in here, when Quinn came to the door.

"Hi," he said.

"Hi." My heartrate shot through the roof at seeing him.

I'd been thinking about him all day, wondering what he was doing. Wondering what our relationship would be now that it was ten years since I'd left him standing outside the hotel while I hopped, heavy-hearted, into a taxi.

That had to have been one of the worst days of my life.

And considering how many times I moved around, leaving behind people I called friends, that was saying a lot.

"I got tied up with my father," he said.

"It's okay." I licked my lips, afraid my voice sounded as unsteady as I felt. Hoping it didn't.

"How was your flight?" he asked. "Lucas Kent, right?"

"Right," I said. "He told me about his company. What he's doing with the whole recycling trash thing is long overdue."

"I agree," Quinn said. "And he's doing really well here."

"He's looking for investors in Dallas," I said.

"I think his company is called Happy Earth Sorting Company."

"It is," I said. "If I had the extra money, I'd invest in his company."

"Yeah?" Quinn said, walking toward me. "Not a bad idea. So I guess Jan left you here to learn our computer program."

"I guess. She didn't really say much."

"That's Jan. But she knows this company inside and out." I pulled out a chair and sat down next to her. He lowered his voice. "I think Momma likes her working here because she doesn't flirt with Daddy."

I laughed before I caught myself.

"I guess that's a good reason."

"As good as any," Quinn said. "So..." He opened his phone. Clicked through. "I've got your username and password here."

With a few clicks, he had me logged into the computer.

"A lot of people," he said. "No. Everyone finds this program complicated."

"Do you find it complicated?" I asked, looking at his square jaw and lips that I longed to feel against mine again.

He turned and looked into my eyes.

"No," he said. "But I don't count."

28

QUINN

The loud sound of jets provided background noise as I sat next to Noelle in what we called the pilot's office.

Most of the regular pilots used this office. We had another office for my brothers-in-laws. And Noelle was worried about nepotism. We were a family-owned and run company all the way around.

Around here, being family was a good thing.

Noelle carried the faint scent of jet fuel.

This was the first time I'd ever thought about jet fuel being sexy.

But when it came to Noelle, nothing was like it was.

She changed everything.

Sitting quietly, she watched as I went through the steps of logging in flight information.

"It takes a while to get used to this program," I said. "so don't hesitate to ask me."

"I won't," she said with a little smile.

"Ready to do yours?" he asked.

"Sure." She slid the keyboard over in front of her. "I think I've got it."

I sat back, crossing my arms, preparing myself for her to get crossed up.

As I watched, though, she went through the whole process. Entered her flight information, then hit enter.

Then, with a smug smile, she sat back and looked at me.

"Well," I said. "You are the first person who's ever caught onto that program that easily."

"It's not that hard," she said. "Pilots shouldn't have any problem with it."

"I agree," I said. "But for some reason, they just do."

"Huh." She shrugged and tucked her hair behind her ears.

This girl. She was not only beautiful, she was brilliant.

I'd known that, of course, but seeing it again in action just stunned the hell out of me.

"So..." she said, with a mischievous little grin playing about her lips. "Do I get some kind of prize for being the only pilot who understands the program?"

Oh. I could think of so many prizes I would like to give her.

"What kind of prize would you like?" I asked, trying to keep from letting her know the direction of my thoughts.

"Since this is Friday, I don't have a flight scheduled for tomorrow," she said. "So I was thinking maybe you could buy me a drink."

"You trust my father not to schedule something at the last minute?"

"He told me he wouldn't," she said. "So, yes, I believe him."

I nodded slowly. I didn't trust my father not to schedule a flight for her at the last minute. But I liked it that she did.

"All right," I said. "I know just the place."

"Good," she said.

"I need to lock up my office," I said. "Give me about five minutes?"

"Take all the time you need," she said.

I appreciated the sentiment, but I planned on coming right back.

Being away from Noelle was the last thing I wanted right now.

Even if it was for five minutes, it was five minutes too long.

29

NOELLE

By the time Quinn and I left the building, everyone else had already gone.

Closing down the office was quickly becoming a habit.

Quinn and I stepped off the elevator and walked outside to the parking lot. There was a chill in the evening air, as it should be for October. The light breeze carried the scent of jet fuel.

It was a Friday night. My favorite time of the year.

Though I hadn't gone to football games since high school, the autumn breeze still reminded me of bands playing, hot chocolate, and first kisses.

The impressions were burned into my brain along with those magical feelings that anything was possible.

I'd kissed Quinn before. Ten years ago. I wondered if kissing him again would feel like a first kiss all over again or if it would feel familiar… like coming home.

He opened the passenger door for me when we reached his car. I smiled at him as he closed the door.

I didn't know what had gotten into me. Asking him for a prize for doing what was my work. And asking him to buy me a drink at that.

I rarely went out for drinks. When I attended social events with my fellow officers, I'd make the expected appearance, then excuse myself.

I'd done the same thing with Quinn last night. But last night I'd had a valid excuse. A long day and a flight the next day.

Truth was, I wanted to spend time with Quinn. I'd not only thought about him all day, I'd never stopped being in love with him for ten years.

Ten years. it was time to see if those feelings were real or if they were more of a fantasy. If they were a fantasy, then I could let him go and move on. Find the right man for me.

If they were real, well… I wasn't sure what I was supposed to do. Finding out if they were reciprocated was no doubt a good place to start.

Quinn pulled out of the parking lot and merged with traffic.

"Did Lucas Kent tell you where the name for his company, Happy Earth Sorting, came from?" he asked.

"No." I shook my head.

"His little girl came up with it when he was trying to explain to her what he was doing."

"That's sweet," I said.

"He dotes on that child."

"How old is she?" I asked.

"Two or three, I think."

"A good age."

He shot me a quick smile.

"Maybe. If my niece is any indication, the terrible twos have nothing on the teens."

I laughed.

"Makenna does seem like a troubled teen."

"I know," he said. "It's strange because she'd had everything. Great parents. Four older siblings. One of her sisters lives on Mackinac Island."

"Ah," I said. "That's what she was doing there. What about school?"

"I don't know," Quinn said. "Fall break, I guess. She may be homeschooled some, too."

I kept my opinion about homeschooling to myself. In my opinion, a girl like Makenna needed to be around kids her own age. I'd seen a lot of military kids who were homeschooled and they tended to get into more trouble than those of us who went to public schools—even if we did move around a lot.

"Where are we headed?" I asked as Quinn got onto the freeway heading south on Interstate 45.

"It's a surprise," he said, with a quick glance in my direction.

I normally didn't care much for surprises. Now that I was out of the military, I was hoping to get away from surprises.

Surprise. You're moving to Alaska.

Surprise. Now you're moving to Alabama.

But with Quinn, everything was turned upside down.

And maybe a surprise now and then wouldn't be so bad.

30

QUINN

I'd had a lot of time to think about the things I'd like to do with Noelle.

Probably an understatement.

When she'd asked for a prize, my brain had automatically gone to one I'd thought about often.

Take her back to one of the places where we'd been before.

Before she knew that I lived in Houston.

I honestly thought she could have figured out that I was a Houstonian if she'd tried. She bumped up against it a few times. Like when she called me a cowboy. And when she asked how I knew about The Big Easy where I'd taken her for a beer.

The bartended knew me and knew what kind of beer to bring me. Noelle could have seen that if she'd wanted to.

I think she hadn't wanted to figure it out. If she had, I think things could have been different.

I never had figured her out though. And God knows I'd tried.

At least now I knew why I hadn't. She wasn't from anywhere in particular. A military brat.

We'd both gone to college in Houston at the same time. I'd

gone to Rice University while she'd gone to the University of Houston.

I'd always believe that fate had brought us together. Just like fate had brought us back together.

"Do you have plans for Sunday?" I asked.

She shook her head. "What kind of plans would I have?"

Good enough as far as answers went.

"Well..." I said, speeding up and changing lanes. "You're invited to Sunday dinner at my family's house."

Even out of the corner of my eye, I saw the alarmed expression on her face.

Damn. Father should have been the one to ask her. Coming from me, it made it look like I was moving too fast.

"Father invites all the new pilots over for dinner. It's one of his traditions."

She let out a slow breath.

"Okay," she said.

I didn't know if she meant okay she'd go or okay she understood why I'd asked. I waited, but she didn't elaborate.

"Okay... you want to go?"

"It doesn't sound optional," she said.

I couldn't tell if she was being serious or not. It was dark and the traffic required all my attention. I decided to err on the side of caution.

"Everything's optional," I said. But I knew what she was saying. She'd literally just started a new job. Refusing to attend a social event hosted by the new boss would be starting off the wrong foot.

"I can make an excuse for you," I said.

She shook her head. "No," she said. "I don't mind. Just don't desert me."

Deserting her was the last thing on my mind. I was thinking she wouldn't be able to get rid of me.

31

NOELLE

My breathed snagged in my throat as we pulled into The Big Easy parking lot.

It was the only place outside of the hotel that I'd known Quinn. The place where we'd first acted on the love that had been growing between us for two weeks.

The fact that he remembered… that he brought me back here warmed my heart.

I hadn't remembered the parking lot being gravel, but it was.

Quinn found a parking spot at the back and turned off the motor.

"Ready?" he asked, looking right at me.

"Sure," I said.

"I'll come around."

I let out a long, slow breath as he came around, opened my door, and held out a hand. As I put my hand in his, every nerve in my body came alive.

Even though I was wearing low heels, it was hard walking on the gravel of the crowded parking lot. Quinn kept a firm hold on my hand as we neared the door.

Jazz music spilled out the door, transporting me back to that night ten years ago.

There was no line tonight. Maybe its popularity had waned or maybe it was just early in the evening.

Quinn paid for two tickets and we got the backs of our hands stamped before stepping inside.

The live band consisted of three young men—playing the guitar, playing the piano, and another on the drums. There was a girl playing the saxophone. The singer was the one playing the guitar, but the girl seemed to be carrying the band.

Only about half a dozen tables were filled and another half a dozen people sat on stools at the bar.

Even as we slid into a circle booth toward the back, Quinn kept his hold on my hand.

"Good evening, Mr. Worthington," a young male said, coming up to our table.

"Hello Antonio."

"What would you like to drink?" he asked.

"Is this the place that specializes in beer?" I leaned over and asked with a little smile. That's what he'd told me all those years ago. I should have known that there was more than he was telling me.

I probably could have figured out that he was from here if I'd tried.

He looked at me sideways with a little crooked grin that scattered my thoughts.

"Good memory," he said.

"I'll have what you're having," I said with a slow smile.

"Two martinis," he told Antonio. "Extra vermouth. Extra olives."

"So," I said after Antonio walked away. "You come here a lot."

"About once a month," he said. "My parents believe in family time. Not just family time together."

Antonio stopped by with a bowl of bar mix.

"So," Quinn said. "Once a month I have an evening out with my father."

"Just the two of you?"

"Yeah," he said. "For the most part, we've kept up that tradition they started when we were kids."

"So you spent an evening with your mother and one with your father every month? How do they have any time together?"

He laughed. "It's not always an evening. It could be a lunch or even a breakfast. My dad and I usually come here, though. Have a beer. Play some pool."

He got quiet then as Antonio dropped our drinks off.

I took a sip of the martini. "This is really good."

"I wouldn't steer you wrong," he said.

No, I thought to myself. He wouldn't. I believed in Quinn Worthington.

Always had.

He leaned close. "When are you going to tell me where your tattoo is?"

32

NOELLE — BEFORE

The jazz music was mesmerizing. Or maybe it was Quinn's blue eyes. Up close I could see that they had little shards of emerald green shooting through them, but from a distance it wasn't noticeable. Or maybe it was just the lighting from the mixture of diffused and bright lights reflecting off the shiny mahogany wood of the bar.

Whatever it was, I could just fall into those eyes and never come out.

"So," Quinn said, his head inches from mine. "Tell me something about you I don't know."

"Ha." I looked away. Watched the bartender mixing a drink. So not everyone was ordering beer. There were a million things about me he didn't know. But he already knew so very much. I had to tread carefully if I was going to stick to my resolve to not get too close to him. To maintain enough distance that I could just walk away from him tomorrow.

But in my heart I knew I was already too close to him.

I was going to walk away from him. But it was going to be hard.

"There's so much," I said, tasting my beer. It was cold. Icy almost. I might could learn to like beer cold like this.

"I'm sure," Quinn said. "Just tell me one."

I shrugged and straightened on my barstool.

"Okay," he said. "I'll go first. I wish I could paint."

"Paint?" I had not expected that. "Like an artist?" It didn't fit with what I knew about him. He came off as the preppy business major that he was.

"Yeah. I'd love to be able to capture the way the light reflects around the room." He caught my gaze. "The way it makes your green eyes sparkle."

Oh my. I had not been prepared to have Quinn flirting with me with this.

I focused on the label on my beer bottle. Ran my finger along the seams.

"You could take a class," I said. "I'm sure you'd be good at it. At anything you want to do."

The music changed to something soft with a low beat. Romantic.

"I tried that once," he said. "It didn't take."

I looked over at him. At his strong jaw with the five o'clock shadow that gave him an unexpected edginess. He could almost pass for a bad boy right about now.

He leaned closer. So close I could feel his breath against my cheek.

I cleared my throat. "I have a tattoo," I said.

"You do not," he said, straightening.

"I do," I said.

"What of?"

"I'm not saying," I said, taking a mini pretzel from the bowl of bar mix.

"Where?" he asked, looking at me with a challenge. "Show me."

"I can't do that." I said, tasting the ice-cold beer again.

"Now I'm intrigued," he said, leaning close again.

That was exactly what I'd been going for.

He ran a finger lightly against my cheek, wiping away the smug expression on my lips.

"If I guess right, will you show me?" he asked.

"No!" I said, pushing at his hand.

But he merely clasped his fingers around mine.

"Want to make a bet?"

"I do not," I said, but my resolve was waning.

"A butterfly?" he asked.

"I'm not telling you."

He was so close now. So close he was whispering in my ear.

"A heart?" he asked.

As I turned and looked at him, I realized my mistake.

He leaned forward just a breath and his lips pressed against mine.

Every thought in my head dissolved. And I knew I was in more trouble than I thought.

The seconds passed as we sat like that, our lips pressed together.

All my resolve shattered.

Walking away from him was going to be the hardest thing I'd ever done.

"Come on," he said, taking my hand and pulling me up.

"Where are we going?"

He put his hands on my cheeks and kissed me.

Then he wrapped his arms around me and picked me up, my feet leaving the ground.

"Let's get out of here," he said against my lips.

33

QUINN

The music was louder than normal. I never came to this bar on a Friday night. The bar scene wasn't something I gravitated toward. In my opinion it could only lead to trouble.

When my father and I came here, it was different. We'd talk business and shoot a game of pool. But we always came on slow nights like Tuesday or Wednesday. Times when there was less of a crowd.

I used the weekends to catch a movie hang out with one of my sisters and her husband or boyfriend, depending on what particular year it was.

Noelle's eyes were wide as she looked at me.

"There is no way you're picking up that conversation again," she said.

I laughed. "It's not the conversation I'm so much interested in as it is the subject of the conversation."

Her cheeks turned pink. I'd actually made Noelle blush.

"You are incorrigible," she said.

"I know. But I think maybe you're trying to avoid answering the question."

"Really?" she asked, sliding an olive off the toothpick.

All the blood rushed to my groin. Was she doing that intentionally? Was she blushing one moment and teasing me with her lips in the next?

Yes. I decided. That was exactly what Noelle was doing.

My flirting had just backfired on me.

I had a whole lot of pent up fantasies I was working with. Not that I'd been a saint over the years, but I had not gotten myself into any kind of relationship that I couldn't get out of at the drop of a hat.

"Well," she said, with that mysteriously husky voice of hers. "I'm still not going to tell you."

I leaned close, my voice low.

"If I guess it, will you show me?"

She glanced at me and shifted in her chair. Shook her head.

I just grinned.

I was going to find out. I was going to kiss every inch of her soft delicate skin and I would find that tattoo.

I sat back and put an arm across the seat behind her. She cut her eyes at me, but I could see the smile playing about her lips.

I backed off. This was one game I knew how to play.

"Besides Houston," I asked. "what's your favorite place you've ever lived?"

"Boston," she said, without hesitation.

"Boston has an Air Force base?"

"I was there as a training facilitator." She swirled her drink. "Training others how to train, basically."

"What did you like about it?"

I braced myself for her to tell me she had a boyfriend there. When people had a favorite place, it was usually a favorite because of someone in particular.

"I liked the winters. They were horrible and beautiful at the same time. Every time it snowed, people got friendly. Like the snow was something magical."

"I never thought of Boston as a friendly place."

"It has so much history. And yet it's modern with its subways. In fact it's a walking city. A blend of old and new, especially walking through Boston Common, that's like no other place I've been."

I loved how her face lit up. My mother, a psychologist, always said that if you didn't ask anything, you wouldn't learn anything. She was so very amazingly right.

"Maybe we can visit there some day," I said.

"Maybe so." She looked at me then and the connection between us was palpable.

And that's when I knew that everything I'd wished for was coming true.

Noelle and I were going to be together.

34

NOELLE

Quinn lived in a two-story condo in River Oaks just at the edge of Uptown. He parked his BMW in the middle of a two-story garage that was the cleanest garage I'd ever seen. He was the first person I'd met who didn't view their garage as a storage unit.

The condo had an open floor plan. A pristine white kitchen with a gas stovetop on the island.

If he had a television, I didn't see it. The focal point of the living room was a gas fireplace that came on when we walked into the room.

Floor to ceiling windows looked outside into the darkness. A private yard if I had to guess.

There was a half-bath and a study downstairs. A tall grandfather clock stood next to the stairs leading to the second floor.

I stopped and looked up at the ticking clock.

"My grandfather left that to me," he said, coming back to stand next to me. "It belonged to his grandfather."

"It's beautiful," I said. "It must mean a lot to you."

"It does," he said. "I think my father wanted it, but he never said anything."

I followed Quinn upstairs. There were three bedrooms and an open area that overlooked the living room below.

He had a little writing desk there with nothing but a notebook computer on it.

He showed me to one of the two guest rooms. It had a large bed with a white comforter and an armchair with a floor lamp next to it.

"I'll bring your luggage up," he said, leaving me alone.

I sat on the edge of the bed and got my bearings.

I don't know where I expected Quinn to live, but this place fit him. It was clean and understated.

He was very kind to offer me a place to stay. But I would have to start looking for a place of my own. I couldn't impose on him like this.

He came across as a private person, much like I was.

A few minutes later he came back upstairs with my suitcase.

"Do you need anything else?" he asked, standing near the door.

"No," I said. "You're very kind to let me stay here. But I'll start looking for an apartment."

"Why would you do that?" he took a step toward me.

"I don't want to impose."

"Noelle," he said. "You can stay here as long as you want."

I felt so much in that moment. I didn't want him to leave. Not even to go down the hall to his own room.

It was like I couldn't get enough of him.

I shook my head. At what, I don't even know.

Then he was standing in front of me, putting his hands on my elbows to pull me close.

"I looked for you," he whispered as he tucked my head against his chest and rested his chin on the top of my head.

"And now that I've found you, I don't want you to go anywhere."

My breath hitched. I'd thought about him so often over the years. But I didn't even know if he remembered me. He not only remembered me, he said he looked for me.

And he wanted me here.

I hadn't expected him to be available if I did ever find him again. The country was a big place. Falling back into Quinn's world was such a surreal thing.

It had to be fate.

With such astronomical odds against it, it couldn't be anything other than fate.

Then he kissed me on the cheek.

35

QUINN

Sunday dinner at my parents' house was an event. An informal event, but an event still.

I couldn't remember a single time when one of us hadn't brought a guest. That's how it was with five siblings. One of my sisters always had a boyfriend or at the least a girlfriend. I was different in that I'd never brought a girl home.

I just hoped they didn't make a big deal out of it.

Father, in fact, was the only person who knew that she was more than the newest pilot of Skye Travels.

By the time we pulled up to the front door, the circle driveway was crowded with cars. "I'm trying not to be nervous," Noelle said, as I parked the car and turned off the motor.

I unbuckled and turned to face her.

She was lovely in her long dress with tights and high boots. She had on a long sweater and her hair hung loose around her shoulders.

She looked about as far from military as a girl could look.

"How do you want to do this?" I asked.

"What do you mean?" she asked, biting her bottom lip nervously.

"I can introduce you as Skye Travels' newest pilot or..." The only way to do something was to just do it. "I can introduce you as my girlfriend."

She took a sharp breath. "What do you want?" she asked.

I never had any doubts about what I wanted, but my father was the one who'd asked her here today. I personally would have waited a week. Let her get her feet under her before subjecting her to the Worthington clan.

But since she was here, I didn't want to hide what we had. I wanted my family to know what she meant to me. I'd shout it to the rooftops if given the opportunity.

I took her hand. "I want you to be who you are," I said.

"And what is that?" she asked.

The love of my life.

"My girlfriend."

She nodded. "Then that's what I want."

I let out a slow breath I hadn't known I was holding.

"Are you sure?" I asked.

"Is your family that bad?"

"No. My family is wonderful and I think you're going to love them. And they're going to love you."

Her perfectly bow-shaped lips curved into relieved smile.

I wasn't lying about either one.

I just didn't know how my family was going to react to me bringing a girl... for the first time.

I went around and opened the door for her.

The temperature was perfect, the sun warm, the breeze cool, and I could already smell the grill. That meant Father was out back grilling something. Probably hamburgers.

It also meant that there was more space for everyone to spread out. All eyes wouldn't be on us all at once.

Not that I minded. But, for God's sake, the last thing I wanted was them to frighten Noelle away.

I took her hand as we walked up the sidewalk to the front door.

Noelle stopped and searched my eyes.

"As much as I want everyone to know that we're together," she said. "I'm still worried about nepotism."

"We're a family company," I said.

"I know." She bit her bottom lip. "It's just… I've only worked here for a couple of days."

She was right. Anyone in their right mind would be nervous.

"Alright." I squeezed her hand, then released it. "I understand."

I didn't care so much about my family. They'd be okay. What I was worried about was Noelle. I didn't want her to feel uncomfortable.

It wasn't a good way for her to start a new job and it wasn't a good way for us to start a new relationship.

"You're right," I said. "Let's wait to tell them."

"Really?" She bit her bottom lip again.

"It's the smart thing to do," I said. "I'll introduce you as Father's newest hire. We'll wait on the girlfriend thing."

She nodded. "Okay."

"Okay."

Together we turned and continued to walk toward the front door. I just hoped we were doing the right thing.

36

NOELLE

I sat on a bench in a back yard that like an oasis right in the middle of Houston.

The swimming pool itself was a masterpiece.

From where I sat, I could see not only a waterfall, but a clear wall of water. The yard was strategically tiered so that one side of the pool appeared to be above ground. It wasn't, of course.

And Noah Worthington was in his element standing at the grill. He was wearing a full white apron with *Grandpa* stitched across the front of it.

He was drinking beer with four other men—three were his sons-in-law and one was his future son-in-law.

Three out of the four worked for him.

Quinn and I had walked through the house to the kitchen where his mother and three of his sisters were gathered, making salads.

His niece was sitting at the breakfast table, headphones in her ears. She didn't say anything, but I knew she watched us when she didn't think we were looking.

They were all pleasant and all beautiful. Quinn had made the introductions quickly, before he ushered me out back.

I balanced a bottle of water on my knees.

After a couple of minutes, Quinn came over and sat next to me.

"Would you like something stronger than beer?" he asked.

"No," I said. "Water's fine."

Then the sister I hadn't met yet came outside with a baby in her arms.

At that point, I realized I hadn't needed to worry about being notice. The baby, Sophia, was immediately the center of attention.

Kade, the baby's father put a blanket on the ground for his daughter and wife.

The three of them sat together on the blanket and although they were only a few yards away from everyone, they seemed to be in their own world.

When the baby rolled over and started to crawl, everyone cheered.

The baby looked at them, then rolled over sat down, laughing.

"I think she's becoming a little extravert."

"Is that something that's learned?" I asked.

"I don't know. You'll have to ask my sister. She's the psychologist."

Maybe I'd ask her later. But right now, just watching them, I could see that if extraversion was learned, this baby would definitely be extraverted.

I wondered what it would be like to grow up in such a large family. One where there were always family around and where the parents always lived in the same home.

It was so very different from the way I'd grown up that I couldn't even begin to fathom it.

"Come on," Quinn said. "You haven't met Madison yet."

We walked over to where Madison sat next to her baby.

Madison looked from me to Quinn and back again.

"Hi," she said.

"Hi."

"Madison," Quinn said. "This is Noelle Winston. She was just hired as one of our pilots."

"Welcome aboard," Madison said.

"This is Sophia, the newest member of the Worthington family."

Looking at me, Sophia laughed and held out her arms.

"I think she likes you," Madison said, picking up her baby and snuggling her close. Obviously not ready to share her.

"What's not to like?" Quinn asked.

His sister narrowed her eyes at him. It was a brief exchange between brother and sister, but it meant something.

I just didn't know what that meaning was.

37

QUINN

After lunch, everyone scattered, like they always did. Father, Kade, camped out in front of the television to watch a football game.

Ainsley and Wyatt headed out. Wyatt had a meeting in Wyoming.

That was the thing about having your own airplanes. A trip to Wyoming was practically like going out to Katy.

Brianna and Jackson headed out, too, not saying where.

Mother, Madison, and Wynter took the baby and went upstairs to put the baby upstairs for a nap.

Makenna disappeared somewhere. Probably her room.

Noelle and I went into the kitchen and sat at the breakfast table.

"You survived okay?" I asked.

"Yes," she said. "You're right. I love your family."

"I won't steer you wrong."

She smiled.

"So… you ready to get out of here?"

"Sure," she said. "But would you show me how to use the scheduling app first?"

She handed me her phone.

She already had the app downloaded.

"Is the account different from the one on the computer?" she asked, peering over my shoulder.

"The first-time log in is different."

"So I have an account?"

"You do…but…" I pulled out my phone and logging into my own app. "I didn't give it to you."

"I see…" she said. "Holding out on me?"

I turned and grinned at her. "If you have everything, you won't need me."

"Like that's going to happen," she said under her breath.

I took heart in that offhand comment.

"Here you go," I glanced at her schedule before handing her phone back. "Wait. You have a flight to California tomorrow."

"What?"

I scrolled down. Checked the details. "You're taking my niece home."

I handed her the phone and looked at her. My father had scheduled that. Sometime this weekend. He hadn't said anything to me, but, of course, he didn't need to.

It would be no big deal for Noelle. She was probably used to flying across the country at a moment's notice. She'd be out and back in the same day. Not a big deal. My own father and sister did it all the time.

The Cowboys made a touchdown and the guys cheered at the television.

"This is a compliment to you," I said. "My father almost always flies her himself."

This attachment I had with Noelle was foreign to me. Something for me to think about later. But we had the rest of the day. And I had an idea.

38

NOELLE

Quinn was just full of surprises. He told me we were going to a museum, but the Butterfly Center was not what I expected.

It wasn't very crowded today. A few families. One with two small children. Mostly teenagers looking for something to do on a boring Sunday afternoon. Had I ever been like that? I just remembered being busy. Studying or working. I started working when I was sixteen. Having a full bird colonel for a father opened all sorts of doors.

We stepped into a rainforest with hundreds of butterflies.

I stopped at the top of a waterfall and just watched the butterflies fluttering about in random patternless flight paths.

It was so absolutely beautiful that it brought tears to my eyes.

And added to that was that Quinn knew me well enough to not only know that I would appreciate it, but he put in the effort to bring me here.

It had been so long since anyone had done anything like this for me. The feeling settled into my core and, closing my eyes, I clutched the rail.

The moist air was soft and heavy on my skin. A young couple walked along the path behind us, laughing with each other. I inhaled deeply, the sweet scent of flowers filling the air.

Then Quinn put his hand on my arm.

I opened eyes to find him leaning toward me.

"Are you okay?" he asked.

I nodded and blinked away the moisture in my eyes.

"Thank you," I said. A heartbeat later, a butterfly softly landed on my hand.

Laughing softly, I gently lifted my hand.

"It's a sign of good fortune," Quinn said.

"I don't think my fortune can get much better." Truly I was the happiest I could remember being in forever ago.

"Surely there's something that you don't have," he said.

I looked into his blue eyes. The emerald green streaks were nestled in the dark blue as he looked softly at me, his lips curved at the corners.

"Probably," I said, although at the moment, I wasn't sure I could stand much more.

The early retirement from the Air Force had been disappointing, I'd found a wonderful job in the city of my choice. I'd been a hair's breath away from choosing Boston, but my fond memories of Quinn won out in the end.

Even though we'd mostly stayed in the hotel and I didn't know where Quinn was originally from or where he'd ended up, something pulled me back to Houston.

And here he was.

The good fortune had already touched my life.

He lightly touched my cheek and ran a thumb across my lips. I closed my eyes again and my lips parted.

"There's nothing I'd rather do than make you happy," he said.

Then he lightly touched his lips to mine.

And my world's axis shifted.

Nothing was ever going to be the same.
I'd found my center.

39

QUINN

Normally I didn't mind Mondays. I didn't have anyone breathing down my neck. Instead I went to my office where I was the boss, at least in the day-to-day world. My father was ultimately the boss, of course, but he handled his things and I handled mine.

But today, I didn't care much for Monday.

I stood at my window looking toward the sky. My eyes hurt from watching her plane until it was no longer visible.

I drove Noelle to the office with a heavy heart. I knew she'd be right back—later in the day—but it didn't stop me from not wanting her to go.

I had fleetingly thought of going with her, but that was just insanity. She had her job and I had mine.

She was a pilot and I had to get used to her traveling. I was still baffled as to how I was so accustomed to the pilot's way of life and yet I couldn't seem to get my head straight when it came to Noelle.

I went to my desk and sat down, but I didn't log in to my computer. Instead, I just stared into space.

Noelle worked at my office and was staying in a room in

my condo. I drove her to work and would drive her home again. She'd met my entire family. Yet it still wasn't enough.

She was like a drug that I couldn't enough of. I inhaled deeply. Accepting it.

I knew what it was. It was from all those years ago when she'd gotten in that taxi to catch a flight. I'd let her go and I'd never expected to see her again. I'd looked everywhere I knew to look for her. Even with an unusual name like Noelle, she was unfindable.

If I thought about it, I shouldn't be surprised at my strong reaction to her. I'd certainly thought about her enough over the years.

Now that I'd found her, I wanted to attach her to me and not let go.

Father came to my office door, stopped, and looked at me.

"Come on," he said. "let's go get some lunch."

I glanced at the clock. "It's not even ten thirty."

"It'll be after eleven before we get there."

"Where's there?"

"The Big Easy," he said. "Come on."

What the hell? I wasn't in the mood to do any work anyway.

We took my car. Father didn't particularly like driving a car. Now if we'd been flying, that would have been a completely different story. The only time he let anyone pilot was when he was testing them out like he'd done Noelle. Hopefully Noelle appreciated that because Father wasn't likely to ever fly with her again until he was the pilot.

We had to wait five minutes for The Big Easy to open the doors for lunch and we were the only ones there for the first ten minutes.

Without asking, Antonio brought us both beers and we ordered burgers and fries.

"So catch me up on you and Noelle," Father said.

I knew there was no point in lying to him. There never was.

Father found out everything anyway. In fact, he usually knew things about people before they knew it themselves.

"I'm not sure how to explain it," I said.

"You introduced her as the new pilot."

I rubbed a hand over my chin. "I know. It was her idea."

"I'm listening," Father said.

"She was worried about the appearance of nepotism."

Father laughed. "I hope you told her that nepotism is best."

I laughed, too and took a sip of my beer.

"I tried to explain it, but I didn't want to pressure her."

"You still feel the same way about her?" he asked. "After all this time?"

I nodded slowly, then met his gaze. "I do."

Father settled back against the chair. "I felt the same way about your mother."

I'd heard the story. How his father blackmailed him into marrying Claire. They'd had one child—Danielle. Father had randomly bumped into my mother at a busy airport.

They hadn't immediately reconnected. She'd tossed him the crumb of a clue that Father had pursued. He'd found her at a conference in New York.

"It's hard to explain, isn't it?" I said.

"It's fate," Father said, with a shrug.

I held up my bottle for a toast.

"To fate," I said.

"To fate."

40

NOELLE

The flight to California was long. Normally I would have used the time to relax and let my thoughts wander. It was a bit like meditation.

I knew pilots who were addicted to flying. Couldn't get their thoughts together without that alone time in the air.

Fortunately, I wasn't like that. In the Air Force, I'd spent a lot of time of ground. Training others how to train new pilots. Using my business degree to some extent, after all.

At any rate, my flight over was not as peaceful as I would have liked because Makenna sat up front with me in the copilot's seat.

She had her air pods in, but I could feel her watching me. With her grandfather being a pilot, she no doubt had some idea what I was supposed to be doing. I had no problem with confidence. I'd flown for Noah himself. But judgement exuded off her in waves.

Or maybe it wasn't judgement. Maybe it was just her general surliness.

The flight itself was smooth and we were about an hour out

of Los Angles when Makenna took the air pods out of her ears and actually looked around.

"Where are you from?" she asked, startling me.

It was the first thing she'd said to me on the entire trip. I'd begun to wonder why she wanted to sit in the cockpit.

Why not just sit in the back and have the flight to herself?

"Nowhere, really," I said. "My father was military."

"Surely you have some place you think of as home."

Did I? "I think of home as being wherever my family is."

Makenna pinned me with her gaze. "Where is your family now?"

"My parents live in Germany."

I didn't like the line of her questioning. It felt, again… judgmental.

"Then why aren't you in Germany with them?" she asked.

I spoke to the control tower to give myself time to settle with her questions.

"Because I like it in Houston." I smiled at her. Trying to be congenial and lighten some of the tension. "And since I'm no longer in the military, I can choose where I live for the first time in my life.

But Makenna didn't let up.

"I think it's not Houston you like," she said. "I think it's my Uncle Quinn."

"He seems nice," I said. "But I didn't know Quinn when I moved here." I said the words carefully. I didn't know where she was headed, but with the look on her face, I had a feeling I wasn't going to like whatever it was.

"He has a girlfriend, you know," she said.

And… I was right.

I glanced at her, then calmly turned my attention back to my dashboard. Calmly, I hoped, at least on the outside. Inside, something in me crashed and burned.

I decided not to respond.

Makenna sat back. Tapped on her phone. "You didn't know."

"No," I said. "I wouldn't have any way of knowing."

Makenna shrugged. "I heard he's getting married next year."

My ears were ringing. I straightened and focused on the computer in front of me. I squeezed the throttle with my right hand and put my left hand beneath my thigh to keep my hands from shaking.

Makenna was just a child. She didn't know what she was saying.

But she would know. Quinn was her uncle.

And she'd just spent the weekend with her grandparents. They must have talked about me. And Quinn. And how Quinn was engaged to someone else.

Time got away as I focused on the control panel and tried not to think about what Makenna had just told me.

I just had to land. To drop Makenna off. Then I would have time to think.

The next two hours were a blur as I landed at L.A., dropped Makenna off, got her into a car, and got myself ready to head back to Houston.

Before taxing to the runway, I sat in the cockpit of the little Learjet as my heart broke into a thousand little shards.

There was one thing I was certain about. I was no home wrecker.

I had about four hours to pull myself together and figure out what I was going to do.

41

QUINN

My meeting with Lucas Kent went well. When I saw that he was flying back from Dallas today, I snagged a quick meeting with him in my office.

Lucas was a likeable man. He reminded me of a younger version of my father. A self-made millionaire. Father was a billionaire now several times over, but like Lucas, he'd started with nothing.

Lucas and I had struck a deal and through the power of technology, I had a printed stock certificate in front of me. One thousand shares in Happy Earth Sorting Company.

With Noelle Winston's name boldly printed on it.

Within a few years, thanks to Lucas Kent's success, I fully expected Noelle to be a wealthy woman in her own right. She could cash it in and spend the money on anything she wanted.

Now I just had to decide when to give it to her. It was going to be hard not to just give it to her right now, but if I saved it, it would be a nice Christmas gift. Or maybe a birthday gift. I'd looked up her birthday on her application. It was next March.

If I gave her an engagement ring for Christmas, then I could give her the stock certificate as a birthday gift.

Or maybe I'd give her a ring now and the stock for Christmas.

Hell, I could just give her everything now.

Not today, though. I needed to plan it. We could go out to a nice dinner and I could propose there. Maybe I'd propose at The Big Easy.

No, I mused. It needed to be someplace that would always be there. Someplace we could visit and reminisce when we got old.

Maybe I'd take her to Boston Common. I'd done my research. It was the oldest city park in the United States.

Since she liked Boston, I decided that would be perfect.

I'd have her fly us up. Just for a weekend trip. Then I'd suggest a walk through Boston Common and go from there.

I'd find inspiration somewhere in the park.

I had to make a trip to Tiffany's first.

So much to do.

Deciding to hold off on giving her the stock certificate, I tucked it into my righthand desk drawer and checked the time.

It was getting close to Noelle's return flight time.

I refreshed my screen and checked to see exactly where she was.

One hour.

I had just enough time to run a quick errand and get back to meet her on the runway.

Then my phone chimed.

MOTHER: *Daddy in ambulance. On the way to West Methodist.*

What? I picked up the phone and dialed Momma's number. It rang, but she didn't pick up. What the hell? She just sent the message. She had to be holding her phone in her hand.

I looked at the message again. West Methodist? That was in Katy. Why there?

I ran through my siblings' whereabouts. Madison was back

in Denver. Ainsley was on an overnight flight. Brianna and Wynter, I didn't know.

I dialed Brianna's number. No answer. Straight to voice mail. She had her phone off. She did that sometimes when she was recording.

That left Wynter. She lived at home with Father and Momma, so if anyone knew anything, it would be her.

She picked up on the first ring.

"I can't talk right now," she said.

"What's going on?" I was standing up now. Grabbed my keys off the desk. Moving toward the door. Everything else forgotten.

"I don't know," Wynter said. "I was out. With Cooper. I just got Momma's text. But she didn't answer."

I skipped the elevator and ran down the stairs.

"Wynter?" I said as I hit the bottom flight. "What's happening?"

"I don't know. Gotta go. See you at the hospital."

The phone went silent as she hung up.

"Damn it."

I sprinted across the parking lot to my car.

Beltway 8 was the quickest way to the hospital from here.

My hands shook as I buckled myself in.

I'd just had lunch with Father. Just hours earlier. He'd been fine.

He'd had a run with prostate cancer a couple of years ago, but he'd beat it. The doctors said he would live to be a hundred.

I merged into traffic and raced down the freeway.

This wasn't happening.

Not now.

My thoughts shut down and I just drove.

42

NOELLE

I would always remember this flight to Los Angeles as the flight to hell and back.

It occurred to me that I hadn't asked Makenna for any details about Quinn's fiancé. One, I'd been too stunned and second, I really didn't want to know.

Just knowing what I knew made me sick to my stomach. Once some of the initial shock wore off, I wiped my eyes and mentally outlined my options.

I could go back to Houston and pretend nothing had happened. Chalk up Makenna's words to just gossip. Something misconstrued. It wasn't out of the realm of possibilities.

But I wasn't sure I was willing to take that chance. I could confront Quinn on it. Ask for an explanation. But that just seemed ugly. It would dissolve all the magical sheen off our relationship if we ended up continuing.

I had another option. I could just walk away.

One of my associates in Boston, a man named Ben, had assured me that working with him was always an option. He had a small company. Only a couple of planes. But, I reminded myself, I wasn't working for the money anyway.

Working with Ben could turn into something or, at the least, it would give me something to keep me occupied while I regrouped and found my next direction.

I felt a little better now that I had figured out what to do.

I'd land and take an Uber to a hotel. I didn't have to worry about the things I'd left at Quinn's condo. It wasn't enough to bother with. I had enough with me—my computer and iPad and change of clothes and basic toiletries. A pilot always planned to spend the night away from home even when it wasn't on the schedule. When I got to Boston I could get anything I needed.

Even with the plan to call Ben when I landed, my heart was heavy. The weight of broken heart was so much heavier than a full heart.

Just yesterday, my heart had been light as a feather at the Butterfly Museum. When Quinn had kissed me, I'd been filled with so many possibilities that I'd been walking on air.

I should have known that something too good to be true couldn't be real.

We'd been reunited for less than a week. I couldn't blame him for not telling me about his fiancé. I'm not sure I would have either if I'd been in his shoes.

I dropped the landing gear as I approached Houston. I bit my lip as I contemplated the possibility of seeing Quinn. I wouldn't say anything to him if I did happen to see him.

The odds were pretty low that I would see him. I'd secure the plane, then go straight to the Uber. I'd complete the flight paperwork from the app instead of going into the office.

Things would be cleaner that way. Easier. Less involved.

My heavy heart pounded erratically as I zeroed in on the runway clearly visible in the darkness below.

The landing was smooth. No problems. The light was on in

Quinn's office, so he was there. He was always careful to turn out the lights when he left the building at night.

But tonight I wouldn't be closing down the building with him. There was no one around when I landed. No one to greet me. I parked the plane and secured it. Then scheduled an Uber. Five minutes out. Apparently the driver was waiting at the airport.

By the time I got to the parking lot, the driver was there to pick me up. Clean and simple.

While the driver navigated the traffic I googled a hotel and made a quick reservation.

Fifteen minutes later, I was in my hotel room. Perfectly and sadly hidden away.

I logged into my computer and scheduled a flight out to Boston in the morning. No reason to hang around here. The sooner I was away from here, the sooner I could put all this behind me.

I secured a commercial flight leaving tomorrow at 8:42 a.m.

Now all needed to do was to get some sleep.

I lay in bed staring at the ceiling for two hours.

The last time my heart had ached like this was ten year ago. The last time I'd left Quinn behind in Houston. This time it hurt more.

Because this time I'd thought we had a future.

43

QUINN

I paced the waiting room floor of West Methodist Hospital. By the time I'd gotten here, my father was already in surgery.

I was ushered into a private waiting room that was designed to look like anything but a waiting room.

Plush benches and armchairs. A television silently broadcasting the Weather Channel.

But the furnishing couldn't disguise the sterile scent and the clean feeling in the air. Certainly didn't disguise the tensions that came with the hospital territory. Draped over it like a veil.

My mother sat frozen on the edge of a bench, her hands clutched together in her lap.

Wynter sat next to her, her heels bobbing up and down, her jaw clenched.

When I'd asked them what was happening, they'd both just shook their heads. Either they didn't know or they weren't able to talk about it.

I found out from one of the nurses that Father was either having a heart attack or was about to have one. Complete arterial blockage they said.

He was having heart surgery right now.

Hours. They said it could take hours.

I wasn't sure I could stand this kind of stress for hours. I was pretty sure Momma and Wynter couldn't handle it either.

But there was no choice.

Since I had to do something, I began calling my other siblings. My grandparents. I didn't know enough to tell them much, but they needed to know what was happening. To get here if they could.

This was different from Father's prostate cancer. Both were serious, but his happened quickly. And it could end quickly—one way or the other.

Two hours later, I had worn myself out.

That's when it occurred to me that Noelle would have landed by now. Oh God. She would be looking for me. I was supposed to give her a ride home.

My hands shaking, I dialed her number. Straight to voicemail. Maybe she'd forgotten to turn her phone back on. Or maybe she hadn't landed yet.

I opened the app on my phone and checked her status. Landed. At least that was one less thing to worry about. She'd find her way home.

I sent her a quick text message.

ME: *Call me when you can.*

Waited for the delivery confirmation, but it didn't come.

The social worker came to the door looking for Father's family. I couldn't worry about Noelle right now. I slid my phone back into my pocket.

"They've started the surgery," the social worker said.

"Just now?"

"They had to make sure he was ready."

Stabilized. I filled in the blanks.

After the social worker went back into the abyss of the hospital, I went to sit silently by Momma.

I needed to pace my anxiety. To be here for my mother. And my sisters.

I took deep calming breaths. Found something calming to center my thoughts around.

Noelle automatically filled my thoughts.

I checked my phone. Her text still hadn't been delivered.

Now I had something else to worry about.

44

NOELLE

I finally had a message back from Ben when I landed in Boston the next morning.

He was in France with his wife for a second honeymoon.

I turned my phone over and stared out the window at the tarmac racing past.

I just hoped I lived to go on a first honeymoon.

The grass is always greener.

I didn't bother telling him I was in Boston. Simply asked him to call me when he got back in the country.

I shrugged. Couldn't complain about a few days to get reacquainted with Boston. I probably needed a break anyway. Not that I'd planned it, but I'd gone straight to work for Skye Travels the day after I processed out of the Air Force.

The teenager sitting next to me hummed to herself as she sucked on a hot cinnamon candy.

What a difference a day made. This time yesterday I was not only flying the plane myself, but I was sitting next to a surly teenager who delighted in telling me bad news.

Apparently the fates weren't ready for me to settle into

place yet. I thought I'd found my destiny with Quinn. But he already had plans.

Thinking about the whole thing made me sick, so I occupied my mind with finding a hotel.

My thumb brushed against the photo app, bringing up a picture of a lovely blue and white butterfly I'd taken two days ago.

My breath caught in my throat. I hadn't told Quinn, but the little tattoo, hidden from daily view on the back of my right shoulder was a tiny iridescent blue monarch butterfly. It had been done by an artist in Germany who did realism work. The butterfly image literally looked as though it had landed on me.

I'd gotten it right after I'd graduated from high school. I'd gone out for a drink with some friends and the tattoos had followed. The guys in my group—there only two of us girls—had gotten tattoos of barbed wire around their arms and tigers, our high school mascot. The girl in our group had gotten a heart on her ankle.

At first I'd said no tattoo, then I'd seen a picture of a butterfly the artist had done and at the time, it hadn't had any particular meaning.

I didn't regret doing it. Not really. Actually, I rarely even thought about it, since I couldn't see it.

Now it had a meaning. Now I'd think of Quinn when I saw my butterfly tattoo.

Now I knew I'd been destined to see Quinn again. Even though it had been too late. He was already engaged to someone else, I'd found him. I knew where to find him now. And, who knows, maybe we'd meet again in this lifetime.

I closed my eyes and waited while everyone else stood up to disembark. No need to hurry the process. Besides, I had nowhere I had to be.

I would take some time to myself. Regroup. Settle myself.

My destiny wasn't determined yet.

I opened my eyes and stared out at the baggage handlers tossing luggage onto a cart. Every piece of luggage had a destination. Someone waiting for it.

I had a destination. I just didn't know what it was. And someone, somewhere, was waiting for me.

I'd always love Quinn with all my heart, but it was time to move on.

I pulled up Quinn's number and blocked it.

45

QUINN

My father made it through the cardiac bypass surgery and was going home tomorrow.

Those two days—the day of the surgery and the day after—were two of the most traumatic days my family had ever experienced.

But we'd come through it. We'd survived.

Noelle had disappeared.

I'd texted and called. But got no response. No answer. She returned with the airplane and then she had just vanished.

Her suitcase still sat in my bedroom.

I thought of all sorts of things that could have happened. She could have lost her phone. Maybe something happened and her family needed her. Germany. Her parents lived in Germany. Anything could have happened. Maybe she was hurt that I wasn't there when she landed and didn't know that I had a good reason. Still...ghosting me seemed like an extreme response.

My concern increased exponentially when she didn't show up to work. Noelle was a veteran. She was responsible. She wouldn't just not show up for work without a good reason.

Work was important to her. She'd even put work above our relationship.

But when I thought back over the time we'd spent together, I knew there was another possibility. She didn't want to be in a relationship with me. I'd kissed her the night before she vanished. She would have thought I vanished.

Still. I couldn't come up with a logical explanation.

I was still a bit edgy and getting over the near loss of my father.

Then I called my niece.

"Hello." I missed the happy sound of her voice. It was a mystery what had happened to the cheerful child she'd been.

"I'm trying to locate Noelle," I decided to skip the small talk with her.

"What do you mean missing?"

"I mean I haven't seen her since she flew you back to California."

"Maybe she crashed."

I held the phone away from my ear. Makenna's name was right there. I'd called the right person.

"Makenna. She didn't crash."

Silence.

I took a deep breath. Why did she have to be so difficult?

"Did Noelle say anything to you? About anything? Was anything wrong?"

Makenna heaved out a sigh.

"She might have been a little bit upset."

"About what Makenna?"

"She didn't know about your fiancé."

"Fiancé?"

"I heard Grandmomma and Grandpappa talking about it."

The rest of the conversation was a blur.

I got nothing else of any value out of her.

But it was enough.

I should have known. Father told Momma everything.

They would have talked about me and Noelle. About how there was only one woman for me.

They would have made assumptions and Makenna would have put her own spin on things. For some reason Makenna didn't like Noelle.

But she didn't like anybody these days.

If Makenna had told Noelle I was engaged to someone, Noelle would have no choice but to take it the wrong way. It was an extreme reaction, but I could see where she could put that together with my unexplained absence Monday night.

There was no telling what all Makenna had actually said to Noelle.

This was a mess and I needed to fix it.

46

NOELLE

Snuggling into my new long wool coat, I stepped out of the subway and headed toward the park. The white clouds were banked and the first flakes of the season's first snowfall were falling.

I turned my face up toward the sky, letting the wispy flakes fall on my face.

It was near noon on a Wednesday morning. I'd been in Boston over a week.

I'd be meeting with Ben tomorrow about taking some flights for him, but other than setting that up, I'd had a leisurely week. It was a strange feeling not having anything to do. I'd had a weekend like that here and there over my life, but never a whole week.

I wouldn't say I could get used to it, but oddly enough, I hadn't minded.

I reached the fountain in Boston Common and stopped to watch the snowflakes landing in the water.

A calmness had settled over me the past few days. I was at peace with myself.

I realized I didn't have to decide my future right away. I could take my time.

A man with a neatly trimmed silver beard, also in a wool coat, walked passed and smiled at me.

I smiled back. This was what I liked about Boston. People said the south was friendly, but I'd found the Boston to be open and accepting.

I wandered aimlessly along the walkway, wondering how things might have looked hundreds of years ago when the city was young.

A man sitting on a park bench a few yards ahead stood up and faced me. I didn't pay him much mind. I just continued my stroll.

Then he stepped out in front of me.

And I was face to face with Quinn Worthington.

I froze, standing a few feet in front of him.

"Hello Noelle," he said, with that little grin I'd fallen in love with.

"Quinn? What are you doing here?"

"Looking for you."

"But…"

"How did I find you?"

I nodded, my head reeling.

"You told me," he said.

I tilted my head to the side. "No. I don't think so."

He took a step forward.

"You told me that Boston was your favorite place out of all the places you'd ever lived."

"I did, didn't I?" A snowflake fell on my eyelashes and I blinked it away.

He nodded. "You did."

I swallowed and forced myself to think.

"I didn't know you were engaged," I said.

"I didn't either."

"Makenna said—"

"Makenna is a troubled teenager who doesn't know what she's talking about." He said the words quickly.

I shook my head.

"I told Father about you. I told him ten years ago that I'd met the only girl for me and I told him he'd just hired that very same girl. I'm sure he and my mother talked about it. They talk about everything."

"I don't understand. Makenna…"

"Makenna must have overheard them talking. About me and you. But she didn't know that you were you. She thought you were someone else."

Unless she was just being mean. He didn't have to say it for it to be true.

He closed the distance between us and put his hands on my arms to pull me close.

"Noelle," he said. "You've always been the only girl for me."

My heart was beating so fast, I wondered if he could hear it.

He tilted my chin up so that I could look into those blue eyes with the emerald green streaks.

"I waited for you," he said.

My breath hitched.

"You waited for me all those years?" Maybe he was insane. "You didn't even know who I was."

"I knew everything I needed to know. I knew that you were my soul mate. And…"

He pressed his lips against mine.

"And?" I asked, looked up at him through my lashes.

"And the day I saw you walking across the tarmac I decided to let you go. To move on. Maybe that girl walking towards me had possibilities."

"That girl was me." I shivered, but it wasn't from the cold.

"Yes. I set you free, but you were already there. You know the saying, right?"

"If you let something go and it doesn't come back, it was never yours. If it comes back to you, it's yours."

"Something like that."

"Noelle," he said. "Will you be mine?"

My heart swelled. I could feel the pieces fitting back together again.

"I've always been yours."

Kissing me, he put his arms around me and I put my arms around his shoulders.

He lifted my feet off the ground and twirled me around.

Then he put an arm beneath my knees and lifted me off the ground.

"Let's get out of here," he whispered against my lips."

Then after another long kiss, he turned and carried me toward the subway.

Loved Reading about Noelle and Quinn?

Turn the page for a preview of Unexpected Vows...

UNEXPECTED VOWS PREVIEW

EMMA BLAKE

Today was going to be a good day.

April weather in Houston was stunningly beautiful. It was still winter in a lot of the country and all of Canada. Take Vancouver, for instance. Today was rainy with a high of thirty-five degrees.

I parked in my assigned spot in the second floor of the garage, grabbed my oversized tote bag and Starbuck's latte, and took the elevator down to the ground floor. I was early, as always, so I was the only one on the elevator. I liked it that way. It was one of the many ways that I avoided small talk.

The door opened and I stepped out, my red-bottomed heels tapping on the concrete. The shoes pinched my feet and scraped the backs of my ankles, but image was everything. Tonight I would reward myself with a hot bath and soak away the soreness. Then tomorrow I would do it all over again.

I could have turned left and walked inside, using the staff elevator to get to my office. Instead, I turned right toward the visitor's entrance. Using the sidewalk allowed me to soak up a few minutes of sunshine before I spent the rest of the day tucked away in my air-conditioned office. Two butterflies flitted around the row of pink and white daisies lining the walkway while a bluebird did a touch and go over one of the half dozen wooden benches.

The usual food truck called *Morning and Noon* sat in its usual place in the parking lot. They had THE best egg and cheese biscuits and lattes that were as good as the one in my hand. Although there was no line yet, I didn't stop. Not having to get my own breakfast or lunch was one of the perks of being a Senior Architect.

"Good morning, Miss Blake," Bob, the doorman said as he opened the door for me.

"Good morning, Bob. Is Harrison here yet?"

I already knew that he wasn't, but I liked Bob. He was a good man.

"No ma'am. Not yet. He'll be here though."

"Uh huh." I slid my shades up to the top of my head and walked inside. "I know." The receptionist, Misty, liked those scented humidifiers, so the lobby always smelled like cinnamon or vanilla and spruce trees during December.

"Have a good day," Bob said.

"You too, Bob."

I pushed the button to go up to the tenth floor. My employer, Skye Designs, occupied floors ten and eleven. There was only one more floor above that—the Skye Travels corporate office. They were the least busy since their main office was at the airport. A waste of good space, but no one asked me.

One of my associates had designed a rooftop work and lounge area and was waiting on board approval. I'd seen the plans and was looking forward to having the outdoor space to use as a place to take a break from my desk. Taking a cue from Las Vegas, he was proposing using an outdoor misting system. With the Houston weather as hot as it was during the long summer months, those misting systems were becoming more and more popular. In fact, I was proposing private patio misting systems as part of my current project design.

Stepping off the elevator, I walked down the hallway to my corner office and dropped my tote bag on my desk. Taking my coffee, I went to the window and looked out over the Uptown Galleria area. This building was on the western edge of River Oaks, giving me a south and west view.

I'd lived in New York for all of eleven months before being recruited to Houston by Skye Designs. I'd established a good reputation based partly on my motto "Less is More." One of the Worthington Enterprises board members, a woman named Ainsley Beaufort, had purchased one of the New York condos based on my designs. She'd liked it so much, she'd offered me a job at her company in Houston.

It was hard to turn down a position as senior architect, especially with the salary they offered. But it wasn't New York, something I was still on the fence about.

A police car pulled up to front of the building and parking. I shrugged. Not my business.

Wanting to get some creative work done before my meetings started, I sat at my drafting desk and did some sketches.

Harrison Moore

Grabbing two egg and cheese biscuits and two lattes from the food truck outside the office, I glanced at my watch. I was still early enough.

As an executive assistant, if I wasn't early to work, I was late. And I had to come with breakfast in hand or there would be hell to pay.

"Good morning, Bob," I said as I hurried through the door he held open.

"Boss is upstairs." Bob's voice held a note of warning.

"I had no doubt," I said over my shoulder, heading toward the elevators.

I punched the button with my elbow and took a taste of my coffee. Not bad. I usually preferred my coffee cold, but it easier to just order two hot coffees.

Getting on the elevator, I punched eleven with my elbow and nearly spilled coffee.

I squared my shoulders and waited for the doors to open.

The tenth floor, like the rest of the two-year-old building was plush and understated. Worthington Enterprises was expanding so quickly and in so many different directions, they had decided to form a corporation and build their own building to house the myriad divisions they were developing.

The top floor was occupied by Skye Travels. The legendary founder of the Skye Travels airline company, Noah Worthington, still came into the office on occasion. And even though it was only on occasion, he had the best office in the building.

A perk of being the founder.

The tenth and eleventh floors belonged to Skye Designs. Founded by one of Noah's daughters, it was one of the newest and fastest growing architectural firms in the country. Texas was perfect for the Worthingtons. Go big or go home could be their motto.

That was one reason why I chose to work here. Another thing the Worthingtons believed in was starting from the ground up. Unless, of course, a person was like Emma Blake who brought their reputation with them.

If you start at the bottom, you know how things run from the inside out, Noah had told me on the day he'd hired me as an executive assistant.

I dropped off one coffee and one biscuit at my desk and knocked on Emma's door.

"Come," she said.

I rolled my eyes. Would it seriously hurt her to say *come in* instead of *come?*

"Good morning, Miss Emma," I said.

She didn't bother to glance up from her protractor.

"Breakfast is on your table," I said as I set the coffee and biscuit on the little table next to one of the floor-to-ceiling windows. Why she didn't work there, I didn't know. If this were ever my office, I'd put my drafting table right in front of this window.

I shrugged when she didn't respond and walked back out.

"Thank you," she said, just before I closed the door behind me.

Emma wasn't all that bad. She expected five hundred percent from everyone, including herself. Always first to arrive in the mornings and last to leave at night, she had no social life. In the four months I'd worked for her, I'd never once recorded a social engagement on her calendar. No personal phone calls. Nothing. Just work. Notwithstanding her hairstylist, personal trainer and nutritionist.

The oddest part about her lack of a social life was that she was a looker. Five four, one hundred twenty pounds, long brunette hair secured at the back of her head with a clip. A heart-shaped face with emerald green eyes and perfectly bow-shaped lips.

Always dressed professionally, I'd never seen her without a suit jacket. And heels. The woman always wore heels.

Sitting at my own desk I ate my breakfast while I checked messages and reviewed her calendar.

Maybe, just maybe, I'd have a few minutes to work on my own project today while she was in a meeting.

Just as I was caught up, a message popped up on my screen.

EMMA: *I need you in my meeting this morning.*

So much for that. I didn't know how I was supposed to ever

be successful with my own project if I was always running after Emma Blake.

Emma

My assistant, Harrison Moore, sat next to me with his iPad open and ready to take notes while we waited for Mr. Jackson Fleming.

Mr. Fleming had a large corner office on the eleventh floor with a perfect view of downtown Houston. He had this office in Houston and one at the airport. He wasn't an architect. He was a pilot.

But he and his wife had founded Skye Designs, so there was no one to complain to about how the office could be better used by someone who worked there every day. Besides, he was the head of Skye Designs.

I used the wait time to check my emails.

"Did you follow up on this question from Robert Johnson?"

"Yes ma'am," Harrison said.

Harrison had been my assistant since I'd gotten here. I hadn't picked him and hadn't asked questions. Whoever picked him had made a good choice.

What I did know was that he was my age and had an architectural degree from the University of Houston. Though it wasn't part of my job description, I planned to begin mentoring him after I got a handle on my own projects.

I also knew that he was far too handsome with deep blue eyes that always seemed to hold a secret smile. By the end of the day he had a five o'clock shadow that added a bad boy sheen to his boy next door looks.

Not that I noticed. He was my assistant. And work was not a dating pool.

With nothing of interest in my email, I locked the phone and tapped a finger against the screen.

"Do you know what this meeting is about?" I asked.

"No ma'am," he said, with a glance in my direction. "You don't?"

"Nuh-uh."

Finally, Mr. Fleming walked in and sat at his desk.

He was always a pleasant man, but at the moment he was wearing a scowl.

I braced myself, for what, I didn't know.

"I've been on the phone all morning," he said, without preamble.

"Is something wrong with the Martin account?" I'd been working on the Martin account since I got here four months ago.

It was a planned mid-rise condominium unit near the Highland shopping center in River Oaks. A labor of love for me. Everything I believed in. *Less is more*. Comfortable housing, designed especially for those who worked from home. No gold faucets that were prohibitive to using. Just high quality and clean lines.

"I'm afraid I have some bad news."

Why hadn't Mr. Martin come to me? If there was a problem with the designs, he should have come to me.

"I can fix it," I said. "He should have come to me."

"It isn't Mr. Martin's account."

I glanced over at Harrison. He shook his head almost imperceptibly.

I forced a smile that I was certain looked fake.

"I don't understand—"

"You're being deported," Mr. Fleming said.

"What? Why? I don't—"

"Your Visa expired."

"No," I said. "I renewed it. I have a letter. The paperwork is in progress."

"I'm sorry," he said. "It was denied."

I inhaled deeply. I could still fix this.

"Okay," I said. "I'll just go to Vancouver for six months. Work remotely. I can reapply and come right back."

Mr. Fleming was shaking his head.

"I already proposed that. They said no."

"You don't know how this..." I said. "I'll go to the Immigration office. Straighten it all out."

"Emma," he said. "This is serious. I bought you twelve hours. They were coming to arrest you."

A knot formed in the pit of my stomach. I'd seen the police car myself. I put a hand to my waist to brace myself.

"Arrest? But... I..." I didn't do anything wrong. I went to work every day. I worked hard.

I hadn't set foot in Canada since the day I'd left for college. Going back to Vancouver wasn't an option. My architectural license was here. In the states.

"I agreed to put you on a flight to Vancouver and fly you there myself."

"They can't do that," Harrison said, speaking up suddenly.

I looked at Harrison. I didn't even think he liked me all that much, but here he was going to bat for me.

Keep reading Unexpected Vows...

Kathryn Kaleigh is the author of over seventy novels, over one hundred short stories, and many collections.

kathrynkaleigh.com

www.ingramcontent.com/pod-product-compliance
Lightning Source LLC
Chambersburg PA
CBHW030337310726
48979CB00001B/69

* 9 7 8 1 6 4 7 9 1 3 7 9 3 *